PATRICIA KEYSON

A YEAR IN JAPAN

Complete and Unabridged

LINFORD
Leicester

First published in Great Britain in 2019

First Linford Edition
published 2020

A catalogue record for this book is available
from the British Library.

ISBN 978–1–4448–4360–6

Published by
F. A. Thorpe (Publishing)
Anstey, Leicestershire

Set by Words & Graphics Ltd.
Anstey, Leicestershire
Printed and bound in Great Britain by
T. J. International Ltd., Padstow, Cornwall

This book is printed on acid-free paper

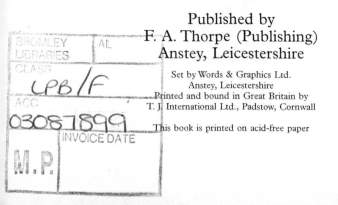

15 JUL 2022

WILKINS

SPECIAL MESSAGE TO READERS

THE ULVERSCROFT FOUNDATION
(registered UK charity number 264873)
was established in 1972 to provide funds for
research, diagnosis and treatment of eye diseases.
Examples of major projects funded by
the Ulverscroft Foundation are:-

- The Children's Eye Unit at Moorfields Eye Hospital, London
- The Ulverscroft Children's Eye Unit at Great Ormond Street Hospital for Sick Children
- Funding research into eye diseases and treatment at the Department of Ophthalmology, University of Leicester
- The Ulverscroft Vision Research Group, Institute of Child Health
- Twin operating theatres at the Western Ophthalmic Hospital, London
- The Chair of Ophthalmology at the Royal Australian College of Ophthalmologists

You can help further the work of the Foundation
by making a donation or leaving a legacy.
Every contribution is gratefully received. If you
would like to help support the Foundation or
require further information, please contact:

THE ULVERSCROFT FOUNDATION
The Green, Bradgate Road, Anstey
Leicester LE7 7FU, England
Tel: (0116) 236 4325

website: www.foundation.ulverscroft.com

A YEAR IN JAPAN

When ex-librarian Emma announces she's accepted a year-long position to teach English in Japan, the news shocks her grown children. Enjoying single life after half a year of estrangement from her husband Neil, Emma can't wait to embark upon her adventure in three weeks. Then Neil is hospitalised after a car accident, and needs a carer at home while he recovers. Emma is the only one available to help. Three weeks — can Neil make up for lost time before Emma leaves, and will she let him back into her heart?

An Awkward Lunch

Emma arrived at Chez Florian and peered through the window. She'd never been to this swish French restaurant before, but her daughter, Ros, had invited her there for lunch as a birthday treat.

A man in a smart black suit held the door open for her and she stepped inside.

'I have a reservation,' she said, 'in the name of Cook.'

'Ah, yes, madam, a table for two.' He led her to a table in a booth which was secluded and looked comfortable. 'Is this suitable for you?' he asked.

'Lovely,' Emma replied. The dishes described on the menu she was presented with sounded delicious and Emma was hungry. She hoped Ros wouldn't be long.

Deciding there was time to nip to the

loo, she took time in there to look at herself. Forty! She couldn't believe she was that age.

The mirror told her she wasn't doing too badly — thick, shiny hair with no traces of grey so far — brown eyes which twinkled when she smiled at her reflection. There were a few lines around her eyes and mouth, but she put them down to laughter.

The mirror wasn't long enough to give a full-length view of her. She knew she'd put on a bit of weight recently, but she didn't care.

On returning to the table, she ordered a glass of wine and sipped it. When the door clanged open, Emma was pleased to see her daughter being led to their table.

'Mum, happy birthday,' Ros said, bending to kiss her cheek. 'Oh good, you've got some wine. Let me order a glass and then we can catch up.'

Emma watched her daughter talking to the waiter and was mesmerised by her attractiveness. Her skin was fair and

2

flawless and her mahogany-coloured hair flowed past her shoulders in casual waves. She was vivacious and talkative and her green eyes were captivating.

'I'm sorry I haven't bought you a present, but I've been so busy at work, I didn't have the time,' Ros said, when they were settled with their wine.

'It doesn't matter at all, Ros,' Emma assured her.

Then she found herself thinking that it did matter. Not the lack of a gift, but that Ros hadn't made time to get something for her. It showed thoughtlessness and Emma didn't like that trait in her daughter. For now, though, she brushed the thought aside.

'Here's to a very happy fortieth birthday,' Ros said, raising her glass and toasting her mother.

'Shush,' Emma said, 'I don't want everyone knowing I'm that age.'

'It's a major milestone. You should be proud to have made it this far and still looking pretty good. Oops, not very tactful, sorry.'

Emma giggled.

'Let's order, shall we? I'm starving.'

'I'm having a salad to start with,' Ros said, without looking at the menu.

'Are you? Well, I'm going to have moules marinieres with some extra bread.'

Ros fiddled with her phone.

'Mum, are you sure you should be having that?' she asked.

'Why? What's wrong with it?'

'I don't like to say this, Mum, but you are putting on weight, aren't you? Don't you think you should cut back a bit?'

'I'm happy with the way I am,' Emma said, 'and I don't think my birthday is the time to ration myself, do you?'

'I suppose.'

'What about a main?'

'I'll have the fish parmentier,' Ros said.

'I'm going to have the roast duck breast with cherry sauce.'

After ordering, Ros checked her phone again.

'Are you waiting for something important?' Emma asked.

'It's this big project at work. If there's a problem they'll contact me and want an answer straight away.'

'You can't even have a lunch break?'

'I am having lunch. But I can only have an hour.' Ros put her phone back on the table. 'I heard from Sam yesterday. It sounds as though my little brother's having a good time in Australia.'

'He's managed to visit so many countries in his gap year. I hope he can settle down at university when he gets back. Do you wish you'd taken a gap year to travel?'

'No, I'm happy. If this project goes well, I should be up for promotion. What about you, Mum? Are you happy?'

'I am. I like living on my own. I can do what I want when I want, eat what I want.' She glanced at Ros. 'It's a kind of freedom. Although I have to admit it was a bit strange waking up on my birthday and finding myself on my own with no-one to share it with. It was lovely of you to suggest meeting for lunch.'

'What about this evening?' Ros asked. 'You'll do something with Dad, won't you?'

'Why would I? We lead separate lives now. I'm meeting up with some friends.'

'Your library colleagues?'

'No. I didn't tell you, after I left my job at the library I went on a course. Teaching English as a foreign language. And I met some lovely people. We're going out for a meal and then going clubbing.'

'Mum! You have changed.'

'I'm teasing. We're having a meal then will go to a wine bar afterwards. But what about you? How are things going? Are you managing to find time for your friends and interests?'

'Work's full on, so I haven't had much free time. I'm desperate to succeed. A lot of evenings I take work home with me.'

Emma couldn't help but compare her to her father. She wouldn't say so, though.

'I'm glad being a management consultant suits you.'

'It was a good choice. And now I want to make an impression. It's a massive project. And you, Mum, what have you been doing since you left work? You're far too young to retire.'

'As you know, after separating from your dad I stayed on at the library for a month working my notice. It gave me a bit of stability with everything else changing. Then I did the teaching course I mentioned.'

'Why? What will you do with it?' Ros asked.

The waiter brought their starters and they began to eat.

Emma hugged her secret plans to herself. She wasn't sure how Ros would react to her news.

'Having a language teaching qualification opens up opportunities all over the world. I found it interesting and I liked learning new things again.'

'Right. Well, that all sounds fine, but I think it's time you and Dad had a talk. You've been apart six months and you must be over your mid-life crisis by now.'

'Oh, Ros, really. Is that how you see it? It was more than that. You'll have to get used to it. Living on my own has given me a lot of freedom.'

'I thought you had a lot of freedom when you were with Dad.'

'It's completely different when you don't have to give any thought at all to another person. I'm having a great time.' Emma pulled out the last mussel with her fork and popped it in her mouth, then she dipped the remaining bread into the garlicky juices and sucked in the heavenly taste.

'Delicious,' she said.

The waiter removed their empty dishes. Ros picked up her phone and checked it.

'I just need to send a text. Sorry.'

Emma was sad not to have her

daughter's full attention.

When their main courses arrived, Ros had finished texting and put her phone down.

'So what now, Mum?'

Shocking News

Emma took a breath.

'Now, I'm going to live in Japan.' She wasn't ready for the look of sheer horror on her daughter's face.

'What? I don't believe it. On your own?'

'Yes, on my own, but working for a language school. I'm only going for a year, then I'll be back.'

Emma hadn't been expecting this sort of reaction to her going away. Usually, Ros was all for women being independent and forging ahead with their plans. Then she realised Ros had an emotional interest in this plan. It was her mum who was going away.

'Does Dad know?'

'Not yet, but I will let him know before I leave. He'll be dealing with the house sale on his own.' Emma steeled herself for what she knew was coming.

'The house sale? You've put our family home on the market?' Ros's face fell and she looked miserable. 'How could you? It's where Sam and I grew up.'

Emma felt sad for Ros. It was her childhood home and, despite everything, they had all experienced happy times there. She understood her daughter's reticence about the sale, but she should face up to the reality of the situation.

'You don't live there any more, Ros. Neither do I and neither does Sam. Your dad is rattling round in it and I'd like my half of the money to buy a small home of my own. A little flat, maybe — like the one I'm renting at the moment.'

Surely Ros could see the sense of that. She waited for her daughter to reply.

Ros ducked her head.

'Everything you've been doing is out of character,' she mumbled. 'You leaving Dad, selling our family home,

11

going to live in Japan.'

Emma reached out to touch her hand, refusing to be drawn into the argument Ros seemed to be directing the conversation.

'I'm very excited about Japan. It will be a different way of life. Can't you be a little pleased for me?'

'And what about Dad? What's he going to do?' Ros looked daggers at her mother.

Emma wouldn't let herself be fazed.

'Work as usual, no doubt. I'm sorry you're upset, Ros.'

'It's all so final. I'd hoped you'd get back together.'

'You can't expect us not to get on with our lives. You and Sam have both moved away and have your own very full lives.'

Ros looked up and nodded her head.

'I suppose. I just wished you'd told me.'

'You're always too busy to talk to or see me. You're quite like your dad, focused on work. I wanted to tell you face to face rather than in a text.'

'When are you going?'

'In three weeks. Now what about a dessert?' Just as Emma asked the question Ros's phone rang.

'Sorry, Mum, I must take this.'

Emma studied the menu and decided on a tarte tatin.

When Ros had finished her call, she grabbed her bag, stood up and kissed her mum.

'Sorry, there is a crisis at work. I must go. I'll see you soon, though.'

Emma kissed her daughter and sighed as she watched her rush out of the restaurant.

Once again she couldn't help but compare Ros to her father and his attitude to work.

Neither of them had sent her a card, either. But she wouldn't let it spoil her birthday even if she did have to pay the bill on what was supposed to have been Ros's treat. In spite of being left on her own she would indulge in the dessert she'd chosen.

As she ate, she thought about her daughter's reaction to her news. It must have come as a bit of a shock to hear her mother was going to Japan, but it was a pity she couldn't have been more pleased for her.

She understood Ros was upset her parents weren't getting on and had separated, but it would make no difference to the way they treated their children. She loved Ros and Sam with all her heart.

She had loved Neil that way once. What a pity things had gone wrong.

Birthday Treats

Leaving the restaurant, Emma decided to forget her family for the moment and concentrate on herself. It was, after all, her birthday. And not just any old one. A milestone, as her daughter had pointed out, which deserved something special, she felt.

So how better to start the afternoon than by shopping?

She walked along the high street enjoying the August sunshine. Steering clear of the usual shops she visited, she side-stepped into an arcade and found a shop selling rather swanky underwear. Why not? Her trip to Japan necessitated new clothes.

Inside the boutique, she found it easy to choose from the array on offer and then asked the assistant if there was anywhere nearby where she could get some up-to-the-minute outfits.

Over an hour later, she was carrying a stack of bags containing just the sort of things she'd never worn before. The colours were brighter and bolder.

Ros had been correct about her having put on weight, but Emma was happy with her new figure. After all those years when she'd thought she ought to cut back, slim down, do this and do that for someone else, mainly Neil, her husband, she realised none of it was really necessary.

She passed a hairdresser's, whose name on the door was familiar, but she couldn't place it, and decided to see if they could cut and restyle her hair.

'Yes, we've just had a cancellation,' the receptionist said when Emma enquired.

'Come through.'

The stylist lifted and combed through Emma's shiny hair and asked if she had anything in mind.

'No, I'm looking for a change and something easy to keep in place.' Emma said. As the stylist took the scissors to her hair, Emma wondered if she should have said she didn't want it too short. Then she decided to leave it in the young woman's hands and relax.

'Your hair is beautifully silky,' the stylist said.

'I don't do anything special to it,' Emma replied. 'By the way, I noticed you have a list of treatments in the window. Are you a beauty salon, too?' Then she remembered where she'd read the name before.

'We do massage, manicures, pedi-cure, that sort of thing. Why, are you interested?'

'It's my birthday today,' Emma confided. 'My son sent me a voucher for a pampering session here.' She thought of Sam and how caring he'd been to remember her birthday when he was away having adventures far more interesting than his mum's day. She tried not to compare his gesture with Ros's.

'That's nice. I'll give you a more detailed brochure before you leave. And happy birthday.'

Any tension left in Emma from the past few months floated out of her as she closed her eyes and thought about coming back here at some stage and being cosseted.

When she opened her eyes, Emma gasped at the reflection in the mirror.

'It's wonderful,' she said. 'I love it.'

'You've great hair to work with,' the stylist said. 'I'm glad you're pleased.'

'About the beauty treatments . . . have you any special recommendations for those?' Emma asked.

'I always think a face massage gets rid of a lot of tension and wakes you up. And a back and shoulder massage is good too. Something on the beautifying side is beneficial psychologically, of course. Say a pedicure? I'll get the brochure.'

Emma left the salon, having made an appointment for a beauty session before she left for Japan, feeling on cloud nine. After many years, she had things to look forward to. Her life was coming together at last.

Strolling along the road, her new hairstyle bouncing around her face, Emma felt thirsty. The café opposite looked inviting, so she went in and ordered a coffee.

While she was waiting for it, she took a look at the cakes on offer. She really shouldn't indulge any more — she'd eaten exceptionally well at Chez Florian. But she still craved something sweet.

A couple of those tiny macaroons wouldn't send her arteries into overdrive, would they? She ordered them and enjoyed her post-shopping snack.

'Hello.'

Emma looked up to see a colleague from when she worked at the library.

'Val, how good to see you. Come and sit with me and we can have a gossip.'

'We miss you. I hope things are working out OK,' Val said, as she sat opposite Emma. She laughed. 'You've been shopping, I see. Anything special?'

'I've been spoiling myself. Do you

like my hair?' Emma swung her head from side to side.

'Lovely. And what have you bought?'

Emma opened the bags so Val could have a peek.

'And I've booked myself a pamper session, courtesy of Sam. And I've had lunch with Ros. A full day and it's not over yet. Plus, I get to see you, Val.'

'Oh, I love the pants.'

'They're not pants, they're lingerie.' Emma giggled.

'And when will you be wearing these beautiful new clothes?' Val asked.

'I'm going to teach English as a foreign language. In Japan.'

'My goodness. You don't do things by halves, do you, Emma?'

Val seemed pleased, but Emma didn't want her to feel she was gloating by going on a trip to such an exotic place.

'I've still got shopping to do. Luggage and other stuff. The weather in Japan is going to be warm when I get there, I think, then there might be quite a bit of rain and the winter holds the possibility of snow. So a mammoth shopping trip — how will I cope?'

Val sighed.

'It all sounds very exciting. Not that life isn't exciting at the library.'

Emma glanced at her and wondered if she was joking.

'I've spent a long time working up to this. I spent years as a teaching assistant when the children were younger and then, when they became more independent, I appreciated having the library work and the supportive colleagues there to help me through my separation with Neil. It gave me continuity, something to get up for when life seemed such an upheaval.'

'Of course, we knew you were doing the TEFL course, but Japan! Wow, that is really breathtaking.' Val put her hand on Emma's arm. 'We were all sorry when you left the library.'

'I wanted a new direction and the English as a foreign language programme has given me the confidence to think that perhaps, when I return from Japan, I could do the teacher training course I always wanted to do.'

'You'll make a marvellous teacher, Emma. I remember when those kids came in to do homework in the library and asked about things. You were always very attentive to them. Put a lot of yourself into making sure they understood what they were learning. And when you led a storytelling session with the younger ones, I was always spellbound. I think I must be your number one fan.'

'Thanks, Val. You're very kind, but I just love imparting any knowledge to anyone. Which brings me to the fact that it's my birthday today.' Emma was keen to diffuse the gush of praise for her which took her by surprise.

'You should have said. Is that why Sam treated you and Ros had lunch with you?'

Emma nodded.

'And why I'm treating myself to these.' She picked up a pink macaroon and bit into it. 'I love them. Here, have the other one.'

Val shook her head.

'First of all, happy birthday. And I would like to treat you to a large piece of cake and anything you'd like to drink.'

'Are you trying to stuff me like one of those poor ducks in France?' As she said it, she felt a bit sick, thinking back to the duck she'd eaten in the French restaurant. She had to put that image to one side.

'Not at all,' Val said. 'I just want an excuse to have something myself, but it's my slimming club this evening and I can't bear the thought of putting on weight.'

'Since I've been living on my own, I haven't worried about that sort of thing. Believe me, Val, there's more to life than striving to be slim. What does your husband say about it?'

'Now you mention it, Stephen, I must say, says nothing about my figure. I don't think he even registers that I go to a slimming group once a week. When I ask him if he thinks I'm fat, he says I'm perfect.'

'Then believe him. What a nice thing to say,' Emma said, wondering if Neil would say a thing like that. Perhaps once upon a time, in the early days of their relationship, but not during the lead up to their separation. 'You're happy with Stephen, aren't you, Val?' she suddenly added.

'Of course, he's my husband.'

That wasn't what Emma was expecting. She was glad her colleague was happy, but the fact she was feeling like that just because Stephen was her husband, she found disturbing.

'What will you have as my birthday treat to you, Emma?' Val wanted to know.

'I'm not indulging on my own, but I don't want you to break your diet rules if you choose to stick to them.'

'What diet?' Val laughed. 'I think a birthday is a good excuse, don't you? I'm having one of those strawberry mille-feuilles. Every time I come in here, I have to look the other way and shun them. Not today, though.'

'Good, they are delicious. I've already tasted one from here and they are fantastic. If you're sure, I think I'd like a slice of the raspberry and ginger tart. The ginger should help with the indigestion I'm sure to get later on.' The two women laughed. 'I'm glad I ran into you, Val. I'm really enjoying my birthday.'

Val ordered another cup of coffee and Emma decided on an iced tea with fruit decorations — a bit like a non-alcoholic Pimms. Very celebratory. She felt special. Nothing could spoil this day.

Disaster Strikes

'Cheers,' Val said, raising her cup. 'Whose phone is that making a noise?'

'Sorry, Val, I think it's mine.' After her time with Ros, Emma felt particularly bad about the interruption.

'Don't you think you'd better answer it?' Val asked.

'I suppose.' Emma rummaged in her bag which was on the floor beside her chair. 'Hello? Hello? I don't think anyone's there. Ah, yes.' Her heart rocked as she listened to the voice at the other end. When the call ended she put the phone on the table.

'What is it, Emma? You've gone ashen.'

'It was the hospital,' Emma said.

'Not one of your children?'

'No, my husband has been in a traffic accident. They've rung me as his next of kin.' Emma was shaking.

'Did they say how badly hurt he is?' Val took her hand and squeezed it.

'They said he's broken some bones and is in a lot of pain. I'll have to go. I'm sorry.' Emma stood up and gathered together her bags.

'Let me come with you. I can drive.'

'That's kind, but I'll be fine, honestly. I'll get a taxi. Thanks for the treats. I've enjoyed sharing my birthday with you. I'll come into the library before I set off for Japan.'

It briefly crossed her mind that Neil might need her and she'd have to forgo her adventure. Then she told herself there was no way that was going to happen. They were leading separate lives and she couldn't feel responsible for his welfare.

She gave her friend a quick hug before leaving the café.

*   *   *

When she entered the A & E waiting room there were a lot of people, but no

27

sign of Neil. She supposed he was already being seen to in a treatment room. A receptionist studied her computer screen for a moment.

'Let's see . . . Neil Cook? He's through those double doors. Turn left and then you can ask at the desk straight ahead for his exact location.'

Emma thanked her for the help and rushed through the double doors.

It wasn't long before she was in a cubicle looking at the familiar face of her husband. His eyes were closed and there were frown lines on his forehead as though he was in pain.

He was wearing his dark brown hair a little longer than he used to, which suited him. He looked diminished on the hospital trolley. There was no sign of the tall, muscular man she had known for so many years.

She wanted to stroke his cheek and touch the dimple in his chin which she'd always loved and found immensely attractive. Instead she simply spoke quietly.

'Neil, I'm here.'

He opened his eyes and she took in their familiar nut-brown.

'I'm glad.'

She reached forward to kiss his cheek, but suddenly felt awkward, especially when he winced and moved his head away. She didn't know if it was because of the pain or because he didn't want any physical contact with her.

'What's happening?' she asked.

'I'm waiting for x-rays. A coach has overturned on the motorway so I think I'm a long way down the queue now.'

'How's the pain?'

'Awful, but better than it was. They've given me strong painkillers. They think I've broken my right arm, but need to check exactly where and how before they put on a cast. Or it might need pinning. And I've probably broken some ribs too. It certainly feels like it.' He took short breaths as if to emphasise the fact. 'It's really painful.'

'Poor you, Neil.' Emma felt genuinely

sorry for him and was sad to see him in such a bad way.

She moved a plastic chair from the corner so that she could sit next to him. It felt natural to take his hand, but she resisted, not knowing how he would react.

His eyes were closed again and she checked her watch. There was plenty of time before she needed to get ready to meet her friends. She hoped he would be sorted out before she had to leave.

A nurse entered the cubicle.

'How are you feeling?'

Neil opened his eyes.

'Not at my best.'

'Is the pain controlled? We can see about giving you some more medication shortly.'

'Please.'

'I'm afraid there will be quite a wait before we get you fixed. Everyone is busy with the coach crash victims. We're assessing them and as soon as that's done we'll slot you in the right place to be dealt with. It's a case of priority.'

The nurse turned to Emma.

'There's a drinks machine down the corridor and a café in the main concourse if you get hungry. I'll be back to check you are OK shortly, Neil.' She patted the bed and left.

'OK?' Neil said. 'I'm hardly that.'

'Shall I tell you about Ros to keep your mind off things? I met her for lunch today. She's very like you, very work focused. I hadn't realised. She kept checking her phone and then had to dash off before we'd had dessert.'

Neil chuckled, then grimaced and laid his left hand on his ribs.

'I don't know how many ribs I've broken, but it's incredibly painful.'

'I'm sure. Anyway, Ros has this daft idea we were having some sort of mid-life crisis. I think she blames me for us splitting up and she's very silly to imagine we'll get back together again. I told her we're selling the house and she

31

was very unhappy about it.'

'I am, too,' Neil said.

'It was the family home and we all have our memories from all the years spent there, but we have to move on. I'm keen to buy a little flat.'

'It feels so final.'

'It is final, isn't it?'

They didn't speak for a few minutes and Emma checked her watch again.

At last a medic came to take blood from Neil. Then, no sooner had that been done, than a porter arrived to take him to x-ray.

'Shall I come with you?' Emma asked.

'I'll be fine,' Neil replied. 'I hope I won't be long.'

'There's a bit of a queue,' the porter informed them. 'Why don't you get yourself a coffee?'

Emma sighed. The air was oppressive and she needed to get out of there. She told a nurse she would be getting a drink and if they needed her they could phone her mobile.

'Fine, Mrs Cook.' The nurse was already occupied with another patient.

★ ★ ★

After nearly an hour, Emma decided to return to see if Neil was back from x-ray. She almost collided with him being wheeled into the cubicle.

'That's one more thing done,' she said, forcing a smile on her face. 'It will be another wait for the results, I expect.'

The nurse came over.

'Just got to check your blood pressure and temperature if that's all right, Neil. How are you feeling?'

'In pain,' Neil replied.

He looked terrible and Emma was desperately sorry for him. All she could do was stand by.

After what seemed like a lifetime, a woman in a white coat approached them.

'Hi,' she said, 'I'm Doctor Warren, one of the team treating you today.

We've got the results of your tests and your right arm and elbow are broken, plus you have a few broken ribs. Are you right-handed?'

Neil nodded.

'Not so good, then. We're going to keep you in hospital for a couple of days just to make sure there's no concussion or lung damage, although the x-ray should have picked that up. Any questions?'

'No,' Neil said. 'Thank you.'

Then they were waiting again. Emma checked her watch and wondered if she could leave. She wasn't helping Neil or the nursing staff by being there.

'What's up with you? Why are you checking the time? Got a date, have you?' Neil asked.

'I'm meeting friends,' Emma said. 'It's my birthday, remember, I had made arrangements. I never expected to spend my birthday in hospital.'

Neil reached out his left hand, but it didn't quite connect with Emma.

'I'm sorry, I forgot. Please go and

enjoy yourself, I'll be fine.'

'I can't leave you until you're settled. What are we waiting for now?'

A nurse came to take Neil's blood pressure again.

'We're hoping to get you a bed on a ward shortly, although I've no idea how long that will be,' she said.

'Emma, please go and have a nice evening out. I mean it, I'll be fine.'

Although it was tempting, there was no way Emma could leave him until he was settled in a ward. It was silly, she knew, as it didn't make a lot of difference where he was. He was being looked after.

'I'll go and get a sandwich and a drink from the machine outside. Would you like anything?'

'No,' Neil said. 'I feel too sick to eat or drink. You go ahead.'

In the corridor Emma sent texts to Ros and Sam to let them know about their father's accident. Then she had a birthday dinner of a pre-packed sandwich and a cup of tepid tea.

Happier Times

It had been late when Emma had arrived back at her flat the previous night, but she knew there was no chance of a lie-in as she needed to get on with the day.

After Neil's broken arm had been set in a plaster cast and he'd been given a sling to wear to support his elbow, he'd been taken to a ward. Then he'd reeled off a long list of things he'd hoped she'd collect for him.

That was her first task and she wasn't looking forward to it. When she'd moved out she'd taken everything she'd needed in one go and she hadn't been back since.

Walking into the hall of the place she'd once called home, she looked around. Nothing had changed.

She wandered into the sitting-room, sat in an armchair and looked out of the window at the back garden. It looked rather unkempt, but pretty with the roses and other colourful flowers in bloom. The grass needed cutting and the hedges had been allowed to grow wild.

She ran her finger over the coffee table next to her and lifted it to look at the dust she'd accumulated. Neil wouldn't notice a bit of dirt and she supposed he hadn't spent much time at home over the past few months. It didn't matter as with any luck the house would soon be sold and another family would be living there.

She stood up and carried on walking through the familiar rooms then went upstairs.

It seemed strange walking into their bedroom. Her bedside table had nothing on it but the lamp. His was cluttered with papers and books and a couple of dirty mugs. She resisted picking them up and taking them down to the kitchen. It wasn't her place to interfere.

Under the bed she found the holdall Neil had said would be there. She put it on a chair and undid the zip, then she went to the chest of drawers.

After pulling open his underwear drawer she reached in and took out a handful. How strange and weird it felt to her to be handling personal things of Neil's when not so long ago it would have been quite normal.

As she stuffed things into the bag she realised it felt as though she was handling a stranger's things. They been married for over 22 years.

Once she'd sorted out the things Neil had requested, she didn't hang about. She wanted to get back to the hospital as soon as she could as she wasn't sure how well Neil was coping.

★ ★ ★

'Here you are, Neil. I hope I found everything you wanted. I'll unpack it into the locker for you.'

Neil tried to shift himself into more

of a sitting up position, but groaned. Emma gestured for him to lie back down.

'Don't move on my account. I can talk to you whatever.' Emma continued with her job.

'Is everything all right at the house?' he asked.

'Fine. I turned the hot water off and made sure everything was locked up. But I should imagine they won't keep you here long. Beds are at a premium. I wanted to bring you some of the roses from the garden, but I wasn't sure if they are allowed.' She looked round.

'There don't seem to be any flowers in here. I brought you your favourite chocolate instead.' She put the Toblerone bar on the overbed table and finished putting his things neatly in the bedside locker.

'I've heard back from both Sam and Ros. Sam said he'd come home, but I told him you'd be fine and wouldn't want him to spoil his trip.'

'I'm not sure when I will be fine, but

I don't want the children spoiling their lives because of this stupid accident.'

'Good. And I'm sure your bones will start mending soon and it will be just weeks before you are back to normal.'

'I can't imagine not being in pain, not being able to move and needing help with everything.'

'Oh, come on, Neil, you were lucky. It could have been an awful lot worse. This isn't like you. You're positive about pretty much everything.'

'Not this. There's nothing positive to this.'

Emma was pleased when a young woman came down the ward and over to them to check his chart.

'You're a lucky man, Neil, having a wife who brings you chocolate.'

Emma decided not to correct her. After all, she was legally still his wife. She thanked the woman and then broke off some of the chocolate to eat.

'What about Ros? What did she have to say?' Neil asked.

'It was just a text. She said she has a work do this evening, but she'll visit tomorrow.'

'Typical Ros, but I do understand her trying to impress by getting this project right.' Neil winced and turned his head away from Emma.

'What is it? Shall I get someone?' Emma was anxious and didn't know what to do.

'I need some painkillers. They pulled me about when they washed me earlier. I asked for something to make the pain more bearable and they said they'd bring it, but they haven't.'

'I'll see if I can find someone,' Emma said, going to the entrance of the six-bedded unit Neil was in and looking up and down the corridor.

There were a couple of nurses at the nurses' station, but one was on the phone and the other had her head buried in a computer. Why weren't they looking after Neil?

'Can I help?'

Emma swung round and came face

41

to face with a young man who was smiling at her. His name badge said he was a nurse called Cameron.

'My husband was hoping for some tablets, he's in a lot of pain. Neil Cook.'

Cameron nodded.

'The drugs trolley is on the way. He shouldn't have to wait too long.'

Emma returned to Neil and explained.

'It's all about waiting, in this place,' Neil moaned.

Emma wanted to deflect his mind from the pain and his bad mood.

'You were talking about Ros wanting to impress.' She laughed. 'Do you remember when she was six and it was her birthday party? She insisted she could eat that huge chunk of chocolate cake and then play on the bouncy castle we'd hired.'

'She was sick.' Neil cracked a smile and Emma was pleased. 'I remember you always cooked fantastic birthday cakes for them. There was a computer one for Sam and a rainbow layered one which Ros was delighted with.

'She insisted it was too pretty to give away to her friends. You looked after them well. They flourished under your nurturing.'

Emma was startled to hear Neil so eloquent about her role in the house. It had always seemed as if he took her role of mother as a given.

'Sam was more reserved. He didn't mind Ros taking the limelight.' Emma smiled.

'Just as well, she wouldn't settle for less,' Neil said. 'They both did well — are doing well.' He leaned back on the pillows. 'It was thoughtful of Sam to offer to come all the way home from Australia.'

'He loves you,' Emma said. 'And so does Ros.' Emma looked at her husband. His eyes were shut and she thought she saw a small tear trying to escape under a closed lid. He'd never been good at emotional stuff.

For some reason, she wanted to hold his hand, comfort him. But she didn't reach out to him. Instead she stayed quiet and thought about the trip ahead of her.

Then it seemed as if everything was happening at the same time. Two nurses entered the unit and were dispensing medicines, much to Neil's relief.

A doctor with his gang, as Emma thought of them, went to the man opposite and a ward assistant was wheeling a lunch trolley along the corridor.

After Neil had been given his pain relief, he seemed more settled, although the tablets would take a while to work.

'We might have to give you injections if these pills don't do the trick,' the nurse said. 'No-one wants you to be in pain. You're doing very well. And please try to eat something, they'll help the tablets work.'

Neil nodded.

'Thank you, I will.'

Emma stayed a while longer to help Neil with his cottage pie and vegetables. In her opinion he could have used his left hand quite well, but he was being a bit awkward and he liked being waited on.

After he'd finished the plateful and had eaten quite a good helping of ice-cream, he appeared more relaxed.

'It's good of you to come and bring the things, Emma. I appreciate it. I'm sorry about your birthday yesterday.'

'It wasn't too bad a day. Pity I had to come here, though. What I mean is, it's a pity you were in an accident.'

Neil reached for her hand, but she moved it slightly.

'You've done something to your hair. It looks good. Suits you.'

Emma was surprised he'd even noticed. She'd almost forgotten the restyling of the previous day. Such a lot had happened since she'd turned forty.

Patient Care

As Emma returned from collecting a cup of tea from the machine, one of the nurses at the nurses' station looked up.

'Mrs Cook, could I have a word, please?' she asked.

'Of course. There isn't a problem, is there?' Emma hoped there wasn't a difficulty with Neil's medical condition. For selfish reasons she needed his recovery to run smoothly.

'I am sure there won't be. I've just been looking at your husband's notes.' She glanced at the computer screen. 'The thing is, he won't be allowed to leave the hospital unless he has someone at home to look after him.

'He couldn't manage on his own at the moment, things like washing and dressing — personal things. I imagine you work. Would it be possible to take some time off to care for him? I know it's tricky. Some employers aren't very sympathetic.'

'We aren't together. We're separated and we no longer live together.'

Emma knew she wasn't being very kind, but being back in the family home with Neil would feel very awkward. It had felt strange enough being there on her own on her quick visit. And, worst of all, the thought of having to cancel her trip to Japan made her heart plummet.

'I see. I'm sorry to have made that assumption. Neil talks about you fondly.'

That astonished Emma. He didn't usually express his feelings or speak lovingly about his family to people he hardly knew. Perhaps it was the effects of the painkillers.

'We didn't want any acrimony,' Emma said quietly. 'Our children might be grown up, but it's better for them if Neil and I are on friendly terms.'

'You do seem like a happy couple. Is there someone else?'

Emma was surprised by the question and shocked that she hoped she hadn't been replaced so quickly.

'I have no idea. He hasn't mentioned he's met someone.'

The nurse smiled.

'I meant someone else to look after him.'

Emma felt embarrassed at her silliness.

'Our son's away, but maybe our daughter could move in with him for a bit. I'll find out.'

'We'd appreciate it. Now that we have the pain pretty much under control, we really need the bed. We always need beds.' She rolled her eyes. 'We'll put a care plan in place.'

'Of course. I understand. I'll let you know as soon as we've sorted someone,' Emma said. How was it that once again she was organising Neil's life for him?

Neil's eyes were closed when she sat down next to him.

'Are you awake?'

'Just dozing.'

'I've been told you can go home if you have someone to help you. Maybe Ros could take some time off to look after you.'

'Huh, as if she's going to do that. And why should she?'

Emma was astounded at the vehemence coming from Neil. How else did he think he was going to manage when he got home?

'Who do you think will look after you then?' Emma dreaded the answer.

He turned his head and looked at Emma.

'Wouldn't you? You've given up your job at the library, haven't you?'

'Yes, but I have another job starting in a few weeks' time.'

He frowned.

'It's very worrying. I want to go home as soon as possible, but the thought of having a stranger in the house with me and helping me wash and dress is awful.'

'The nurses are strangers and they're doing those things for you here,' Emma pointed out. She was starting to feel annoyed with his attitude. It seemed he would only accept one person to look after him and that was her.

'It would be different in our home. I'd rather struggle on my own than have a stranger or strangers there. Can you imagine?'

Emma could imagine and knew she would hate it if she were in a similar position.

'They won't let you go home if there is no-one to care for you, then you'll be a bed blocker and you don't want that. And it's not *our* home any more.'

She tried to keep the irritation out of her voice.

'You need to start seeing it differently. We're selling it, remember? Anyway, that's irrelevant. We need to think who is going to look after you. I expect you could employ someone. There must be agencies who deal with this type of thing. I'll look on the internet for you, if you like.'

She could feel her dream adventure

slipping from her grasp. Once again, she was organising his life, making things easy for him, making things run smoothly.

'Could you postpone starting your new job until I'm better?' Neil asked.

Why should she? Jobs couldn't just be shuffled around to suit Neil, and neither could her life. Emma was furious.

'I'm flying out to Japan to teach English for a year.' There, she'd told him.

'You're what?'

'Going to Japan to teach mature students. I always wanted to teach and this is just the start of my new career, my new life. I know I was a teaching assistant for many years, but it wasn't fulfilling and neither was my job at the library.'

Neil appeared to slump into himself as he turned to look at her.

'I'm very sorry for that, Emma. You never said much to me about it. It was a pity you had to give up your dream of being a teacher.

'I can remember how excited you were about doing the teaching course. Then when you got pregnant with Ros there wasn't much choice but to give up your place. At least I asked you to marry me! I did the right thing! Not all young men would have done that. Remember I was young, too. Just starting out on my career.'

Emma's mind went back to the time she had found out she was pregnant.

'I suppose you could have run a mile and left me to deal with the baby on my own. But we were in love and it seemed natural for us to marry and bring up our child together.'

The early years together had been a wonderful, special time. They'd adored each other.

'I always thought being a teaching assistant suited you. You seemed happy with your work,' Neil said.

'It was good in that I was working with children and it fitted in with our two, looking after you all and the house, but it wasn't really what I wanted to do. And now I have this fantastic chance to teach in Japan. Who knows where it will lead.'

Neil's eyes were closed again, so she sat quietly for a bit.

Then he opened his eyes, reached for her hand with his left one and held it loosely.

'We were happy once, weren't we?'

Emma squeezed his hand.

'Very. We were in love.' She let go of his hand. 'That was then, though, and now I'm forty I am especially keen for a change and I want an adventure.'

'I see. You've changed. And it's more than just that lovely new hairstyle. You seem independent and feisty. How have you found it these last six months?' He sounded gloomy.

'Mainly good. It was a bit strange at first not having someone to share things with, but we hadn't been doing much of that anyway. It was pretty much a lone existence. I mean for the past few years we hardly ate or slept together. We might just as well have been living separately.'

'As you know my work's been full on. It's become more time-consuming the more successful I've become,' Neil confided. 'They give me the biggest potential contracts and I have to go out and make sure I get them signed on the dotted line. It's such a great feeling when I succeed.'

This was the longest time Emma had spent in conversation with Neil for a very long time.

'You're passionate about your work. I envy that,' she told him. 'That's what was missing from my jobs. I want to feel that passion. I'm very excited about this chance to live in Japan and I really don't want to give it up.'

'And especially not to look after me.'

'It's not that,' Emma said, although she really didn't want to get trapped back in her previous life. 'They won't give me a second chance if I let them down. They're relying on me to go.'

'Even if it's an accident in the family?

It doesn't sound like a caring organisation. Surely there'd be some leeway for that.'

Emma sighed. She didn't want to get into all of this, not now, not ever, and especially not in a hospital ward.

'I don't know, Neil. Maybe if we were still together they'd feel some sympathy, but I told them I didn't have a partner or dependent children.'

'No baggage, then.' Neil had a sullen look about him.

'Please be happy for me.'

Neil struggled to sit upright and shook his head.

'Sorry, I'm being selfish. But I want to go home and I want it to be you who comes with me. I'd feel relaxed with you. You know you're the only person I'd feel comfortable with.'

She patted his uninjured arm.

'I know. Isn't it good that we can still talk easily with each other? I'm sure a lot of separated couples can't do that. In many ways it's been easy to separate. It's worked out fine with you staying at the house and me renting my tiny flat. I like living on my own.'

'I don't. And I miss you such a lot, Emma.'

Emma felt the urge to laugh.

'What? You mean you miss all the jobs being done — your washing and ironing kept up to date so that all your clothes were ready to wear, food in the fridge and meals cooked, the house clean, and garden tidy. And all the finance and paperwork dealt with, the bills paid, correspondence done. Is that what you miss about me? That's what it felt like towards the end of our time together. As though I was just a housekeeper.'

'It didn't feel like that to me. I loved you as my wife. I could have been a better husband.'

Emma decided to change the subject.

'Thank you for being co-operative about sharing out our savings. It's made a big difference to me. For a start I was able to afford the TEFL course. And now I'm splashing out a bit on things to take with me, clothes and small gifts for people.'

'I'm pleased for you being able to take up this challenge. Is that why you're going? For the challenge?'

'Yes. It's a great opportunity and one not to be missed. The adventure I long for.'

'This past six months since you moved out and we've been apart has seemed a very long time to me.' Neil sounded wistful.

It felt to Emma that although she had fallen out of love with Neil, he still appeared to like her being around and to have feelings for her.

A Confession

Emma needed some time away from Neil and the cloying atmosphere of the hospital. She'd told him she wanted some fresh air and would have a walk around the hospital grounds.

He hadn't objected, but he'd asked how long she would be. She answered that she had no idea, but would be back. He'd closed his eyes and Emma felt she was being dismissed.

There was a delightful garden near the rehabilitation unit and Emma found it peaceful walking around smelling the flowers and herbs planted in a sensory plot. She found a seat in the shade and sat contemplating her plans for the next few weeks.

This time yesterday she had been shopping for the trip of a lifetime to Japan and here she was today, knowing she would be persuaded into being a nurse/housekeeper for her estranged husband. There was no way she could get out of it, she felt sure. But she was not giving up her dream. She would still go to Japan, whatever happened.

Feeling calmer, Emma returned to the hospital ward and Neil.

'It's a beautiful day. Pity you can't go outside and get some air,' Emma said.

'I've been waiting for my painkillers,' Neil said. 'They're late — again.'

His mood hadn't changed. Emma sat down on a chair by his bed.

'How did the accident happen?' she asked. 'You don't have to talk about it if you don't want to, but I'd like to know. Was anyone else involved?'

'No other vehicle was involved and it was only me who was injured.' He couldn't meet Emma's gaze. 'It was my fault. I lost concentration while I was thinking about my latest mega-deal. Just a split second was all it took.' He looked embarrassed.

Emma was cross.

'You are obsessed with that wretched

photocopier firm you work for. Why can't you take time off from thinking about it? You always have been driven to succeed — no, not merely succeed, surpass success.' She took a breath and calmed down a little before she spoke again.

'That was part of the problem. When I wanted you to stop and spend time with us you insisted on carrying on to achieve even more.'

Emma remembered the emptiness of being without him when it seemed as if he was working 24 hours a day every day of the week. She resented it and him for doing it. A thought came to her.

'Have you been in touch with your work about this or the insurance company yet?'

Neil shook his head.

'I haven't been able to tap out stuff on my phone. It's really painful, Emma. I'll do it when I get home, I expect.'

It wasn't like Neil to put off doing that sort of thing, especially communicating with the market-leading photocopier firm he worked for.

'Shall I do it for you? Where do I find the contact details?'

Eagerly, Neil told her.

'Thanks, Emma, that's a worry off my mind. You'll have to let the company know I'll be out of commission for a few days.'

'Weeks, Neil, weeks,' Emma said.

He looked downcast.

'Are you sure?'

'Absolutely.'

There was an awkward silence between them until Neil's face lit up.

'Hi, Ros, come and give me a hug — well, a gentle one, please.'

Emma was surprised to see their daughter stride into the unit. She looked a bit pale and Emma wasn't sure if it was because she was upset that her dad was injured or because she'd been overworking.

'Dad, I'm really sorry you're hurt. You'll be fine soon — you know nothing gets you down for long.'

'I think this might,' Neil said,

explaining how he wouldn't be allowed home without someone to look after him.

'Neil, here are your tablets,' a nurse said, coming over to him. 'And I have to take your blood pressure and temperature.'

'We'll wait outside,' Emma said, pulling Ros with her into the corridor.

'What's this about Dad not coming home? He's only got a broken arm, hasn't he?'

'He can't manage to wash and dress himself independently and he won't be able to prepare meals for himself. Of course, he could have shopping delivered, but think how you would cope if you had broken bones and were in pain.

'Things like answering the telephone or the door. Stuff we take for granted when we're well. He needs someone to help him,' Emma said.

'Well, I can't look after him, obviously,' Ros said. 'I've got this big project on as you know and it's taking up a lot of time. I have to make a good impression if I'm going to get promotion. Anyway, it's up to you to look after him.'

Emma couldn't believe what she was hearing, especially from Ros.

'I'm not putting my life on hold just because your father lost concentration thinking about his work.' She told Ros the details of the reason for the car crash.

'That's not like Dad. He's usually in complete control,' Ros said. 'Anyway, you're his wife, Mum, you should look after him. It's your duty. You'll have to cancel your plans and stay at home to look after him.'

'My duty? That doesn't sound like your feminist principles, Ros.'

Ros stuck her chin up defiantly.

'I'd tell Dad it was his duty to look after you if the roles were reversed and you'd been in an accident.'

'Do you think he'd look after me or do you think he'd carry on with his work?' Emma asked, narrowing her eyes.

Ros went quiet and then stomped off

back to Neil. Emma followed.

He wasn't looking happy.

'One of the people from what they call a therapy team has been to see me, briefly, and says I will need someone to prepare meals and help with washing and dressing. Well, we knew that, didn't we, Emma?'

Emma sighed, all the peace and tranquillity gained in the garden squeezed out of her.

'All right,' she said. 'I'll do it for three weeks, then you'll either have to manage on your own or with outside help. I'll let the nurses know you can be discharged as I'll be at home to look after you.'

She didn't look at Ros and didn't dare tell her she might have to look after her father. Emma would not delay her plans just because Neil couldn't stop thinking about his work and crashed the car. Work always seemed to come first with him — and Ros.

★   ★   ★

The rest of Ros's visit passed uneventfully. Father and daughter chatted together, but Emma didn't pay a lot of attention to their conversation. She was busy thinking about the coming days. There was an awful lot to do.

'I'm off now,' Ros said, getting up out of her chair. She kissed Neil on the forehead. 'I hope you feel better soon, Dad. Ring me if you need to.' And with a quick hug and kiss to Emma, she was off.

'What a whirlwind,' Neil remarked. 'It was good of her to visit, though. From what she's been telling me, she's planning and executing the current assignment very well. Some of me must have rubbed off on her.'

Emma wasn't sure that was a good thing or not, but didn't refer to it.

'I must be going soon, too,' she said.

'Emma, it was good of you to volunteer to look after me when I get home. Do you really mean it? I know it will be a chore for you.'

'I said I'll do it and I will, but there

will be a lot of preparation for my trip and I won't be with you all day every day.'

Emma watched her husband as he leaned towards her. She softened as she remembered the old days when they'd been close, and smiled at him.

'I don't want you to suffer, Neil. I'll look after you, but I'm going to Japan as arranged. Don't forget that.'

Neil smiled back at her.

'Thank you, Emma. I'm grateful. I'll be better when I'm home, less grumpy.' He reached his good hand to his head and tousled his hair. 'I hate being in here and in pain. And if I have to go through another night with that chap opposite snoring and the one over there keeping on ringing his bell for attention, I'll discharge myself.'

They laughed. Then Neil gripped Emma's hand and his face was serious.

'Emma, I don't want you to give up your dream. You'll get to Japan as planned.'

Sad Reminders

A stressful day followed. Emma had to turn her life round for Neil. While he remained in hospital being cared for, she had to reorganise things for him.

She started by packing a suitcase and bags with the belongings she thought she might need over the next three weeks. If she forgot anything she could always return to pick it up. In fact, she thought, a few hours' retreat by herself at the flat might be a welcome change from caring for the invalid.

After loading up her car she grabbed some shopping bags and headed for the supermarket.

The smell of coffee and bakery products emanating from the café as she walked in caused a delay. While enjoying a berry smoothie and chocolate brownie, she made a list of food they might need. At least they'd be eating together now. Feeling revived, she headed down the aisles.

Back at the house, she felt she might never have been away. She unloaded the shopping, remembering exactly which items went where, then contemplated her next task — beds.

It was a given that they wouldn't be sharing a bed, so where would they sleep?

She decided it might be easier if Neil slept downstairs to begin with. She really didn't want to sleep in the marital bed and chose the spare room for herself.

After unpacking her things and putting fresh linen on the bed, she leaned on the window ledge and looked out at the garden. It was looking beautiful in the summer sunshine, and lush after the rain they'd had overnight. She promised herself time out there later, either weeding or just sitting and reading or dozing.

Then she took time to wander round all the bedrooms. Sam's and Ros's rooms were full of their bits and pieces.

She wondered if Sam would want to live with either her or Neil again. Ros definitely wouldn't and she'd need to clear her room before the sale.

Emma decided she and Neil should discuss which of them would store Sam's things. Then she stepped into their bedroom. When she'd packed Neil's things for the hospital, she hadn't fully taken in the state of the room.

The duvet was in a crumpled heap half hanging on the floor and a pile of discarded clothes sat in the corner of the room. Couldn't he even put his dirty washing in the bin, she asked herself. Although the temptation to tidy the room was great, she resisted and simply left and closed the door.

She supposed that once Neil felt ready to move upstairs she might have to sort the room a bit, but until then it wasn't her place to tidy his mess.

She felt a little awkward, as though she'd been prying on Neil, but she'd have to get used to being familiar again with him and the house.

Collecting some more linen from the airing cupboard she went back downstairs and pulled out the bed settee before making it.

The sitting-room was a pleasant room with a bay window looking out on the lawn and shrubs at the front of the house. Neil would be all right there for a few days at least and it would save him being in pain having to pull himself up the stairs by the banisters. And it would be handy for the downstairs cloakroom.

Emma sat on the edge of the bed. She'd loved living in this house. It had been perfect for them. With four bedrooms, plenty of room downstairs and the large garden to play in it had been wonderful for their family.

She liked the tranquil neutral colour scheme in this room. Neil had left her to the interior decoration of the house so everything was her choice. She wondered if he'd liked it. Perhaps he hadn't even noticed.

She'd insisted on having a real fire, but now the fireplace looked dirty with uncleared cinders and ash. He'd clearly had a fire, perhaps on a chilly evening in spring after she'd left, but had given no thought to clearing the grate out afterwards.

No more nostalgia, it's time for lunch, Emma told herself.

It felt strange working in the familiar kitchen with all the things she'd used for very many years. After preparing a large plate of salad, Emma stepped out on to the patio and sat on one of the garden seats.

The patio furniture was a bit mucky with cobwebs and bird droppings. The place had definitely gone downhill during her absence.

In spite of that, she enjoyed her lunch, listening to the birds singing and the bees buzzing in the yellow rudbeckia. Butterflies danced round the buddleia flowers. This would be her haven when she was finding being with Neil too stifling.

She took her plate back into the kitchen and put the kettle on. While waiting for the kettle to boil she wandered round the house again.

In spite of everything still being there, apart from a very few bits and pieces she'd taken to the flat with her, there was some indefinable difference. She was unable to put her finger on it until suddenly she realised. It smelt different. It used to smell of the children, Neil's aftershave, her cooking and the cleaning stuff she used. All of those aromas had been erased and it didn't smell like home any more.

★   ★   ★

In the afternoon, Emma went to the hospital to visit Neil. He wasn't by his bed, but a nurse explained a physio-therapist was walking him up the corridor.

'We don't like people staying still for long in here. He's doing well. It'll be easier when he's home.'

Emma sat and waited for her husband's return. It wasn't long.

'Emma, if I'd have known you were coming, I wouldn't have gone for a walk.' Neil sat down heavily and nodded at the woman accompanying him. 'It's very painful,' he complained.

'You must move, Neil,' the physiotherapist said. 'I've got a few exercises printed off for when you go home and, of course, the rehab team will visit and advise you. I'll leave you now.'

'Thank goodness,' Neil whispered to Emma, who giggled.

'I've been getting things ready at home,' Emma said, the word 'home' sounding a little strange to her.

'You'd better take these with you,' Neil said, thrusting the exercise programme at his wife. 'Lose them, if you can.'

'Oh, Neil, why are you behaving so badly? I would have thought you'd want to get better.'

'If I thought for one minute that taking a walk would help the agony in my upper body, I'd do it, but it isn't and so I'm not going to.'

He looked a bit like one of the children when they were younger and in a paddy. From experience, Emma knew there would be no reasoning with him.

'I'd best get back, then. Still a bit to do to get ready for you. See you tomorrow.'

'I can't wait. Thank you.'

★   ★   ★

Back at the house, things were taking shape and Emma felt ready to have Neil home. It had been both a physical and mental adjustment, but she'd tried to be philosophical about it.

It could be problematic for both of them to occupy this space together again and for Neil to be reliant on Emma's care. As far as she could see, she'd done all she could for that day. Everything was in place for him to come home.

Deciding on an omelette for dinner,

Emma prepared it and sat in the kitchen, opening a bottle of wine and pouring herself a glass. Then she cleared the kitchen and went upstairs to her room.

She took her laptop and checked on emails before having a deep, luxurious bath. Her flat only had a shower and she was going to make the most of being back in this house.

Back Home

Emma slept deeply and woke refreshed. It took a few minutes to realise where she was, but, as soon as she did, she slid out of bed and padded downstairs to make tea.

It was a glorious morning, the sun already up and shining. Feeling hungry, she poured cereal into a bowl adding milk and sugar. She wondered what Ros would say if she counted the spoonfuls of sugar which went into her tea and on to her breakfast.

Now she thought about it, Emma did feel a bit uncomfortable around her tummy. Even her pyjamas were beginning to strain. Perhaps she should cut back a bit — later on when she didn't have the worry of Neil.

The hospital phoned to confirm Neil would be brought home by the hospital transport vehicle that morning, but there was no way they could say exactly what time he would be with her.

It didn't matter when he arrived. Emma was pleased they'd offered transport as she hadn't looked forward to having to manoeuvre him in and out of her car without adding to his discomfort, and he'd often been critical about her driving. It would have got them off to a bad start.

Emma had a quick shower and dressed in jeans and a T-shirt. Her hair still looked good and she was pleased she'd had it done. She must remember to book in for a trim before she went away.

*   *   *

It was around mid-morning when a vehicle pulled into the front drive. Emma had been weeding the front garden and she got up, wiped soil from her trousers and went to meet Neil.

'Welcome home,' she said. 'Take my arm.'

'You two carry on and I'll bring the luggage,' one of the attendants said, holding Neil's bag. 'I see you're up for sale.' He nodded towards the For Sale sign in front of the house.

Neil scowled.

'Looks like it,' he said.

'Let's hope it won't be long before someone snaps it up,' Emma said.

'Looks a nice place,' the transport man remarked. 'Wish I could afford somewhere like this.'

Emma thought back to when they'd first bought it. It had been expensive, but Neil had insisted they would have enough money for the repayments and they'd already saved a substantial deposit. Perhaps that had been the start of his obsession with working long hours.

At the front door, she helped Neil inside and took the bag from the driver.

'Thank you,' she said.

'You're welcome. Hope you recover quickly, Neil. And I hope you have a quick sale of the house. Cheerio.'

Once inside the house, they automatically went through to the kitchen where Neil sat on a chair looking out to the garden.

'I'm not looking forward to this house sale,' he said.

'Why not?' Emma asked. 'I can't wait for it to be over.'

'Because I like living here. And I can't say I like the idea of people swarming over the house telling me how they're going to rip this out and alter that. If it's so awful then why even consider buying it?'

'Neil, no-one's expressed an interest yet.' Emma was exasperated. 'Come on, this isn't like you.'

She knelt down in front of his chair. If they were to live together for three weeks, they might as well try to do it in harmony.

'What is it? What's bothering you?' she asked.

'It's just something else to deal with at the moment along with this injury. I don't like it when things don't go according to plan and I can't control what's happening. It's not something I'm looking forward to.'

Emma wasn't sure if he meant he didn't want to move from the house or if he was feeling overwhelmed by things.

No Progress

'Let's have a coffee first and then how about sitting out in the sunshine for a bit?' Emma hoped to lift him out of his mood. She hadn't seen him like this before. He'd always been positive and sure of himself, full of confidence and energy.

'I might just go to bed. Getting up and down stairs will be hard, but I suppose that's one of the reasons they insisted I had help.'

'Don't worry about that. I thought you'd sleep on the bed settee in the sitting-room for a few days, then we can start thinking about you going upstairs.'

'That was a kind thought. You're a very caring person. I feel useless. I'd like to do some work. I have a lot to deal with at the moment. Maybe you'd help me, although I'd have to explain everything to you. It's probably not worth it. Probably not even possible.' He sipped the coffee Emma had put in front of him.

'I'm a quick learner. At least that's what I was told on my course. Have a biscuit. They're your favourite.' Emma held the opened packet of chocolate digestives out to him.

'You remembered.'

'Of course. You don't just wipe out over twenty years of memories.'

'I know.'

They sat in silence and Emma stared into the garden.

'The people at the hospital made a mistake,' Neil said.

'Really? What sort of a mistake?' Emma asked, alarmed.

'I should have been kept in hospital for longer. They sent me home too early because they wanted the bed, but really I'm not fit enough to be here. Look at me. I can't do anything.' Neil appeared anxious.

'You big wuss,' Emma teased. 'You'll be fine. You can at least walk. What's the point of being in a hospital bed when you can be comfortable at home with all your familiar things around you?

'You said the hospital told you that as soon as they can organise it the therapy team will be in touch with you about your rehabilitation. But your recovery is mainly just a matter of patience and time. You can treat it as a sort of holiday.' As soon as she'd said it she knew it had been the wrong thing to say.

'A holiday! That's the last thing I want right now. I have several big deals which need a little tweaking and they'll be in the bag. I might lose my job over this.' Neil fidgeted in his chair.

'Don't be ridiculous. You are valued much too highly for that. They'll understand.'

'This is the worst possible time for me to be an invalid. I don't want to be one.' Neil was cross.

'You have to accept the situation you are in and deal with it. We can't change what's happened so all you can do is everything possible to make a full recovery.'

Emma hoped her optimism would rub off on Neil, but he seemed determined to be down.

'How can I pretend to be on holiday when I'm in such agony?'

'Oh, Neil, I know you aren't suffering from something like man-flu and your broken bones are very painful, but you do need to be more positive.' Emma knew his pride was wounded, too. 'Having to rely on me for your basic needs is hard. I know that, but again it has to be accepted. Come on, let's sit in the garden for a bit and you can tell me what you've been doing over the past few months. Then we can have our lunch outside.'

'It will be nice to eat together, Emma. I suppose I ought to think of the plus side of the accident. It's brought you back to me.'

'Only for a short time, then I'll be off. Let me help you up and we'll go and make ourselves comfortable in the sun. It will make you feel a bit better. Perhaps we'll have a little walk round the garden first.'

Emma helped him up and let him take her arm for support before they strolled round enjoying the sights, sounds and smells. She couldn't remember ever doing this with Neil before although she was sure they must have done early in their marriage. When they returned to the chairs on the patio Neil was more relaxed.

'It's good to be outside. I don't spend enough time outdoors.'

'What about your cycling?' Emma was curious.

'I haven't done much of that lately. I've been too busy.'

'Why?'

'I've no idea what you mean.'

'I mean why have you been too busy? Why exactly have you devoted yourself solely to work?'

'There were a lot of opportunities to make sales and I just grabbed them. I like the feeling when I get a contract signed. And I didn't have much to come home for — a ready meal and the TV.'

'And cycling. That's what you did when we were together.'

Emma felt resentful that cycling had kept them apart and now he didn't appear to be bothered about it at all.

'I'll probably get back to it. But it won't be for some time with all my broken bones.'

After lunch, during which they chatted about the current news rather than personal things, Neil yawned.

'I'd rather like to go indoors now and have a lie down.'

Emma helped him to the sitting-room and he made himself as comfortable as he could lying on the bed settee. She sat in an armchair and caught up with e-mails and texts. Soon she could hear deep breaths and she knew he was asleep.

She crept out of the room and back into the garden. She got some tools out of the shed and set to work in one of the borders.

It didn't seem long before she heard Neil calling for her. It reminded her of when one of the children had been ill and she had been for ever running up and down stairs with drinks and words of comfort.

Unhurriedly she tidied the tools away, went in and washed her hands before going into the room.

'Where have you been? I called ages ago. I thought you'd gone out.'

'I was in the garden, doing a bit of tidying. I came as soon as you called. What's the time? My goodness, you've slept for a couple of hours. The time flew by. How about we watch a film on TV?'

'Emma, it's time for my tablets. There's a list of what I'm to have and when. It's all in my bag,' Neil said.

Emma hadn't given his medication a thought. Fine nurse she was. Neil looked pale and he was trying to sit upright, his eyes closed with the effort.

She hurried to help him.

'Lean on me,' she said, putting an arm around him, hoping she wouldn't increase his pain. 'Good, now let me ease you over to your good side — if you've got one.' She smiled at him. 'I'll put this soft pillow under your bad arm.'

'That's much better. Thanks, Emma. Now, my pills. Please.'

'Of course.' Emma went in search of his bag and located the envelope from the hospital. She went back to Neil with the tablets and a glass of orange juice. 'Here, swallow them down.'

Neil did as he was told.

'I'm sorry I'm such a bother, Emma. Never been any good with pain, have I?'

'You didn't do too badly when you fell off your bike and landed in that ditch in Swindon,' Emma reminded him.

He laughed.

'I remember that. I was trying to be a hero for the children's sake. Ros was sure I was going to die.'

Emma was pleased to see vestiges of Neil's old self assert themselves and hoped he'd turned a corner. Perhaps he'd just needed the sleep.

'Shall I put the telly on?'

'I never thought I'd become a daytime telly viewer. How depressing. I feel about ninety.'

'What shall we do, then? I've packed up the gardening stuff and won't do any more until tomorrow, weather permitting.'

'What's for dinner?' Neil asked, yawning widely.

'No idea. I haven't thought that far ahead. What do you fancy?' Emma didn't want to be tied to the kitchen during her stay there, but realised they'd both have to eat. 'I bought a few of what used to be our staples. We had eggs for lunch, so I suppose we could have spaghetti Bolognese or something.'

'And how do you imagine I'm going to eat that?' Neil frowned at her, his good humour gone. 'Really, Emma, don't you think at all?'

What Emma wanted to do was storm off anywhere away from her husband. How could he treat her like that? He'd never been that rude even during the latter part of her time at home. But they had led separate lives then. She almost wished she hadn't offered to look after him. She took a deep breath.

'I'm going to make a fish pie,' she said. With an excuse to leave the sitting-room, she went to the kitchen and made herself a cup of strong black coffee.

Emma managed to stay out of Neil's way until it was dinner time.

'I'm going to serve up in a few minutes,' she said. 'Do you need help to the cloakroom?'

'Please.'

With Neil comfortably settled in an armchair facing the television and his dinner on a table in front of him, they sat eating.

'Nice pie,' Neil said, forking some into his mouth. His eyes were on the television and he laughed at some comic sketch he was watching. The programme was of no interest to Emma, but at least it meant there was no need for conversation. She was still cross with Neil.

'It's quite cosy, isn't it, eating in front of the telly? What's for pudding?' he asked, when the programme finished.

Emma reflected that he was quickly reverting to his old selfish ways. The spark of niceness she'd witnessed a little while previously had vanished.

'Ice-cream,' she said, getting up to take the dirty crockery out.

When they'd finished their meal, Emma made coffee and they sat watching the television once more.

'I hope you're feeling a bit better now you're home,' Emma said.

Neil took his eyes from the screen and looked at her.

'Not really. I hadn't realised I would feel this rough once I got back.'

Emma had hoped that once Neil was out of hospital, things would progress. But he seemed uninterested in being positive about almost anything. And he was showing his old insolent and selfish tendencies which she didn't like or approve of. It couldn't just be the injuries.

Emma decided to delve a little deeper. She went and sat next to him on the end of the bed settee.

'I know you're worried about work, Neil, but things will settle down in a few days and you'll be able to take a more rational view. Perhaps the tablets are making you anxious. Did they mention that at the hospital?'

'No, and I'm not anxious. I'm trying to get better, but you seem hell-bent on nagging me.'

'I don't mean to do that at all. Tell me, what are your plans when you recover?' Emma asked. 'Will you take things more cautiously and spend fewer hours working and spend more time relaxing?'

Neil shrugged his shoulders and then winced with the movement.

'Why should I do that?'

'So you don't get so wound up and lose concentration again. It could have been a far more serious accident than it was.'

'Yes, I know, and I'm not proud of what happened. I can't imagine my life without the work I do. I really enjoy it and am stimulated by my competitive instinct. I've always had it, Emma.'

'Yes, but it's increased considerately.'

'Maybe, but I'm not going to change, I can't live without my work.'

Emma realised the conversation was going nowhere so changed the subject.

'When you're ready, I'll help you wash and get into your pyjamas.'

When he was ready for the night, Emma settled Neil in his bed with a drink and his night-time tablets by his side, the remote control in his good hand.

'Thanks, Emma. Despite what I might have said, I'm glad you're here to look after me. I know I've said it before, but it is quite like old times, isn't it?'

Emma groaned inwardly and went up

to the sanctuary of her bedroom. Opening up her laptop, she looked at details of her trip to Japan once more, just to remind herself there was something brighter on the horizon.

If she'd been at her flat, she would have spent time socialising with her friends from the TEFL course, but as she was stuck here with Neil, she couldn't just pop out to meet them.

She texted them to say she missed them and hoped they were having a great time whatever they were doing. She hoped she hadn't made a mistake by offering to look after Neil.

Out of Character

When Emma woke the next morning the sun was streaming through the gap in the curtains, but in spite of that she felt as though a black cloud had descended.

Her conscience told her she should look after Neil until he was better, but she was soon going to catch a plane to what she saw as a new life of excitement and adventure. He definitely wouldn't be fully recovered by then.

After cooking some scrambled eggs and toast, and making tea, she knocked on the door of the sitting-room and went in.

'Good morning, Neil. I've brought breakfast.'

He poked his head out from under the duvet and groaned.

'I've had a terrible night. I didn't sleep at all.'

There was no point in contradicting him. She put the tray down and pulled open the curtains, letting the light in.

'I'm sure you'll feel better after breakfast and a wash and shave. You can doze all day. You have nothing to do but recover. Let me help you sit up. I've cut up your toast so it should be easy to eat with one hand. There, how's that?'

'Eggs again? It looks nice though. I've been having cereal since you left. It's quick and easy.'

'Scrambled egg is quick and easy too. It's nourishing as well. I'm trying to build you up. If you feel up to it before I leave I'll show you how to make it. And poached eggs.'

'I can't bear the thought of you leaving. I don't know how I'll manage.'

'You'll have other help and anyway you'll be back to your usual self by then.' She sat with him while he ate his breakfast and then helped him wash and shave.

'I think I'll go back to bed now and have a sleep. I'll take some tablets and maybe the pain won't be bad.'

'OK, I'll look in and check on you on a regular basis, but I thought I might give the house a bit of a clean and tidy, ready for anybody who wants to view.'

'I'm not sure about that.'

She knew he meant selling the house, but chose to misunderstand.

'I would have thought you'd be very pleased to have a clean and tidy house. It's looking a bit grubby.' With that, she left the room and closed the door.

She didn't really feel she should be doing the cleaning, but she wanted the sale more than Neil did and was prepared to work hard to get it.

By the time she was ready for a coffee, she'd made progress, but was annoyed with herself for feeling she had to do the domestic chores.

She'd been making a food shopping list in her head and would go and stock up that afternoon. If she bought more staples, they would help the person or people who cared for Neil when she'd left.

And she fancied an afternoon off. She knew she hadn't been looking after Neil for long, but it was starting to feel like a life sentence.

After making lunch for Neil she checked he would be all right on his own and set off. She giggled when she realised how excited she was at the thought of going to the supermarket.

The house had started to feel oppressive and she hadn't made any progress with her plans for Japan. There was quite a lot of preparation still to do.

A friend was going to be living in her flat while she was away and her landlord, having agreed to it, had asked for the necessary information about her friend which she needed to send.

She must also finalise her accommodation in Japan. Details of a couple of potential apartments had been sent to her and she must reply saying which one she preferred. She also hoped to arrange get-togethers with various friends and relatives to say goodbye.

As she shopped, she watched couples

and how they were together. Some were chatting and laughing, others arguing over what to choose and others weren't speaking at all. As she and Neil hadn't shopped together often, it was hard to remember what it had been like.

A little seed of unease was growing and worrying away at her. Neil's behaviour was out of character and she had no idea what was wrong with him, apart from the broken bones and worry about work.

Wanting to make the most of her shopping trip and not feel it was yet another domestic chore she had to take on, Emma headed for the café.

She treated herself to an iced coffee and a strawberry tart. Her phone trilled with incoming text messages as she sat down at a table by the window.

A couple were from friends at the TEFL course, sympathising with her for not being able to enjoy her birthday night out with them and wishing Neil a speedy recovery.

Sam had sent one as well. He said

he'd sent a text to his dad, but doubted he'd pick it up if he was feeling a bit crook. She smiled at the Australian word. Her fingers itched to reply to her son, but what could she tell him? There was no point in worrying him when he was too far away to help.

She put her phone in her bag and bit into the tart. They could become habit forming — unlike food shopping. There was no longer an excuse to put it off, so she drank her coffee, collected a trolley and began.

As she wandered around the store, she reflected that she was still pandering to Neil. She'd always done it to him, but not the children. They were self-sufficient in that they could shop and cook for themselves, knew how to keep a clean and tidy house and were good at prioritising things.

So why couldn't Neil do simple household tasks? Because she'd waited on him, that's why. It was her own fault. The realisation was depressing. If she failed to get Neil to cook a bit, at

least the team the hospital had fixed up
would get him to prepare a meal.

Rubbing Along

'There was a phone call,' Neil called, as soon as Emma walked through the door laden down with heavy bags.

'Who was it?' she asked.

'No idea. I couldn't answer it, could I?'

Not bothering to ask why not, Emma checked the answer machine, but there was no message. She went through to the kitchen to put the shopping away.

'Can you make me a cuppa while you're in there?' Neil said.

Clenching her teeth, Emma stood up from stacking tins in a lower cupboard and banged her head on the side of the worktop.

'Just give me a minute,' she called.

'And my tablets, I need them.'

'You get the tablets and I'll bring the tea.' Emma waited for a refusal, but none came. She filled the kettle and went back to the car for the remainder of the shopping, which she stowed as quickly as she could.

'Here you are,' Emma said, putting the mug of tea next to Neil. 'Have your tablets. Still in pain?'

'Of course I am. It won't just vanish into thin air, Emma.' Neil reached for the mug and spilt some tea on the table.

Emma was on her way to get a cloth when the phone rang. It was the estate agent wanting to arrange a viewing for the following day.

'Yes, ten o'clock will be fine. Thanks.' She hung up and turned to Neil. 'Good news. Someone's coming to view the house tomorrow morning.'

'I can't deal with it,' Neil said, rubbing his left hand over his forehead.

'You don't have to,' Emma told him. 'I'll make sure you're up and dressed in plenty of time and then I'll show them around. They won't be here long. Then the rest of the day is completely free.'

'It's too much upheaval. Think of me

for a change, Emma.'

'That's a bit unfair, Neil. I've done nothing but think of you and cater and pander to you for the past few days.' Emma didn't mention the years she'd done it before they separated. 'If we want to sell the house, we've got to let people see it.'

'I'm not sure I want to sell it, not at the moment anyway,' Neil said. 'I can't deal with people traipsing through our home and having to field phone calls from the estate agent.'

'I'll be able to do most of that if that's what you want.'

'I don't want any involvement. I can't be bothered with it all. What I want is for the house to be taken off the market. Ring that estate agent back, cancel the viewing and tell him we're no longer for sale. And he can come over and take down his wretched sign from the front garden.'

Neil turned away from Emma and she guessed he was sulking. If it wasn't a bit worrying, it would have been laughable. But this definitely wasn't like Neil.

After a few moments Neil turned to face Emma and reached out his hand to her.

'I'm sorry,' he said. 'I don't know what's the matter with me. I keep snapping at you and you're being a ministering angel and putting up with me.'

'Perhaps it's the shock of the accident. Do you think that could account for your mood changes?'

'I've no idea. I don't feel right, but I'm not heading for a breakdown if that's what you're suggesting.'

'No, Neil, please don't let's fight. I'm not finding fault with you, just trying to understand so we can resolve things.'

Neil smiled at Emma.

'It's not too late, is it?'

Did he mean too late to stop them breaking up or too late to come to an amicable agreement for the present?

'What I suppose I'm trying to say is that if we're in close and intimate

105

proximity to each other for the next couple of weeks, we should aim to be agreeable.'

'I'll try,' Neil said, squeezing her hand with his. 'But, Emma, I still feel very uncomfortable about the house sale. People coming in, you know?'

Emma didn't really know, but they'd reached a turning point and if they got on better during the time spent at the house, it would be an improvement.

'OK,' she said, 'I'll ring him now.'

Emma was disappointed as the sale would have been a further distancing of her from her husband. She'd grown to hate the house because of the animosity in it between the two of them, not just since Neil had come out of hospital, but before she'd moved to her flat.

Discussion Time

As she peeled potatoes, Emma thought about her conversation with the estate agent. He'd been sympathetic about Neil's accident and hoped he could be of service selling their house when the time was right. He'd also said he would arrange the removal of the sign which would please Neil.

She was determined to stay positive in spite of her situation and in spite of Neil's low mood. She breathed in the smell of lamb, garlic and rosemary emanating from the oven. Knowing they were usually served with beef, she still mixed up a batter to make Yorkshire puddings.

With a variety of vegetables and tasty gravy, surely Neil would enjoy the meal? Then she decided to make an apple crumble, and prepared custard to go with it. Comfort food, she thought.

But who was she trying to comfort — herself or Neil?

When she took his tray with the full plate of roast dinner to the sitting-room, he was watching a quiz show. Seeing the meal his eyes widened.

'This is wonderful, Emma, my favourite. And you've done Yorkshire puddings.'

'I'd forgotten it was your favourite. It's probably not the best meal to have on a sunny summer's day. I don't really know why I chose to make it.' To fill my time, she added silently, to feel as though I'm really caring for you, to prove I can still cook a roast dinner.

'I'll turn the TV off and we can really enjoy our food without any distraction.' He pressed the off button on the remote.

Emma wondered if that meant he didn't want her to chat either. He seemed a bit more upbeat and she didn't want to spoil the mood. She fetched drinks, apple juice for him and wine for herself, then collected her dinner and sat in the other armchair.

'I suppose I can't have wine because of the medication?' Neil asked.

'That's right, but that apple juice is local and tastes good.'

Halfway through eating, Neil put down his fork and looked at her.

'I'm touched by this gesture, Emma. I haven't had this meal since you left.'

Emma hoped he wasn't reading too much into it.

'There's no way I'd attempt to cook it,' he continued. 'When I've been in, I've had a microwave meal for one.'

'I did notice there were a few of those in the freezer. You were never keen on domestic tasks, were you?'

'Not really. Remember when the children were still here and we had wonderful Sunday dinners?'

'Of course. The good old days.' Emma didn't want to dwell on the past.

'It was a great time when we were all together and sharing things. And you always cooked something delicious for me when I was working late.'

109

'Working late? You were always working late. I never saw you. You worked too hard and didn't know when to stop.' Emma knew she should have kept quiet. There was no point going over the same stuff again and again.

'I was trying to make money, to care for you, and to provide a secure future. I was considered successful at work and received good bonuses. I thought I was doing the best for my family. We had a nice house and didn't want for anything.' Neil continued eating.

'Do you know how I felt? Sometimes I thought you wanted to get away from me. That you didn't want to be with me and the children. I suppose you were well-intentioned, but you became obsessed. Even on family holidays you kept in touch with work.

'I remember several years when you came home early to deal with something. I was always left to pick up the pieces and explain to the children why you weren't around.'

She could still remember the sadness

they'd felt when he'd left them, how an element of the holiday was missing.

'I took you for granted. Why didn't you tell me how you felt? Maybe I could have changed,' Neil said.

'I doubt it. The problem was we never seemed to discuss things fully, did we? You carried on with your work and I was a home-maker and looked after the children. We drifted apart and seemed to have nothing in common. And your hobby took you away from me and the children when you did take time off and could have been with us.'

Emma sipped her wine. It was good they were talking about why their relationship had gone wrong. Maybe it would enable Neil to move forward with his life.

'I loved cycling — especially the races because they were challenging. And my cycling group are a good bunch to be with. I must let them know what's happened and tell them when I might be able to join them again.'

Emma almost clapped with delight.

111

He'd made a positive statement. He was actually looking to the future when he'd be better. 'You've always had a competitive streak. I think it's torn us apart. But latterly, we barely ever ate together and we hardly ever went out or away. Can you remember the last time we went away?'

Neil thought for a moment.

'No, but what you don't understand is that with work I was eating out and staying in hotels. Because I had too much of that with my job I just wanted to be at home when I got the chance. You must see that.'

'I sort of do. But what I don't understand is why even when there was the chance to be with us, you were either off cycling or working at home.

'When the children left home it got worse. We seemed to drift apart even more. It upset me that we didn't even share a bed most of the time. You either came home late or worked far into the night, or should I say early mornings, on your computer.'

Emma didn't admit to having felt lonely in those last months when she'd lived with Neil. It was funny that living on her own she rarely felt lonely.

'I didn't want to disturb you when I was ready for bed. I was being thoughtful rather than unkind.'

'Whatever the reasons, we fell out of love, didn't we?'

Neil shook his head.

'I never fell out of love with you.'

This wasn't something Emma wanted to hear, so she concentrated on eating her food.

'Sorry if I said the wrong thing at the wrong time, but you did ask,' Neil said after a few minutes. He raised his glass. 'I think we should raise a toast to our future. Our future.' They clinked glasses.

'Whatever separate paths our lives follow,' Emma added. They sipped their drinks, then Emma started collecting the dirty crockery to take through to the kitchen.

Neil got up and picked up his plate.

'I'll take this,' he said.

Emma was pleased he was being helpful, but was unsure if he'd manage. Torn between telling him to leave it to her and letting him struggle, she kept quiet. Seconds later there was a crash from the kitchen, followed by a curse.

'Don't worry, it's only a plate,' she said, hurrying to pick up the broken pieces.

'But the mess. I can't even carry a plate without dropping it.'

'Never mind, Neil. Please don't worry, I appreciate that you helped. You go back and sit down and I'll bring the pudding in.'

'Did you resent the fact you had to give up your place at university when we got married?' Neil asked later, when they were sitting with cups of coffee.

Emma smiled as she remembered the time. She shook her head.

'Not at all. I was very happy when I found out I was pregnant and we both agreed we wanted to get married immediately. I desperately wanted to be a teacher, still do, but having Ros and Sam were highlights in my life.'

'Mine too,' Neil said, putting his cup on the table. His forehead creased. 'The responsibility terrified me at first, but you were always so capable, nothing fazed you. You took things in your stride even when you were so ill through your pregnancy with Ros. I loved you so much.' His voice cracked as he said the words.

Emma couldn't help herself getting up and going over to him. She put a hand lightly on his shoulder.

'I never realised. You covered it up well.' It was incredible to imagine he had been frightened at what he was taking on. 'You should have told me,' she whispered.

'You had enough to contend with.' Neil took her hand.

The severe morning sickness she'd experienced had been an ordeal, she remembered. But Neil had experienced problems, too, it seemed. He had been out forging ahead with his job, trying to

115

generate money for a home for his family.

When he came home in the evening, she had tried to be brave and play down her suffering. If only they'd talked to each other and shared their feelings about those things.

Emma looked at her husband and familiarised herself with his dark brown eyes. He had a few grey streaks through his thick dark hair, but that added charm, in her opinion.

As he continued chatting to her, Emma was mesmerised by his melodic voice, she always had been. It was his physical presence which had first attracted Emma to Neil and she was astonished to find herself captivated by his magnetism now.

Promises Made

Emma spent the night tossing and turning and woke from a fitful sleep with a headache. The way she'd felt the previous evening had unsettled her. Her life with Neil was over, she told herself. There was no going back and she didn't want to go back to the way their marriage had been.

She dragged herself out of bed, gulped down a couple of painkillers, showered and dressed, and only then was she ready to face Neil.

'How are you today?' she asked, hoping he wouldn't have noticed her feelings of warmth towards him the previous evening.

'I didn't sleep well. I don't think our chat last night helped. It all kept churning round my head. Our failed marriage. The end of our lives together.' He looked miserable.

She sat on the edge of the bed settee.

'We'll both deal with it in our own way. You'll keep yourself busy with work and I'll teach and study for my teaching degree. We can keep in touch. We'll have to because of the children.'

'You mean we can be friends.'

'Yes.' It was time to change the subject. 'So, what do you fancy for breakfast?'

'I'm not feeling hungry. You have what you want.'

'You have to eat, especially with the medication. How about granola and yoghurt?'

'I'll try to eat some.'

While preparing breakfast, she decided that later on she would search on the internet to see if she could find a reason for Neil to be acting out of character.

In spite of everything that had happened, she wanted to leave him in the best possible health. She couldn't help caring for him.

When their dishes were empty, she fetched tea, and toast and marmalade.

They sat in silence and Emma planned her day in her head.

'Right, I'll clear up the breakfast dishes and I'll help you get washed and shaved. Then we can start our day. I've got a plan for this morning.'

Neil groaned.

'I thought I'd stay in bed today. My ribs are aching and my elbow is hurting far more than it should be.'

'No, Neil, the people at the hospital said you have to get up and do as much as you can. The painkillers should start working soon.' Emma realised her head was no longer aching. 'They do work, you know.'

'They're probably not strong enough. I'm worried about work, too. Did you send that e-mail about the accident? There should be a reply by now.

'As it's a company car they'll need me to make some sort of statement about what happened. Although, how I can admit to losing concentration I don't know. I'm sure they're wondering if they can fire me. That's why you haven't heard anything.'

'I haven't checked my laptop yet this morning and I expect they have other things to deal with too. I doubt your accident will be their number one priority.'

'Exactly. I'm just a small cog in a big wheel. I don't matter.'

'Come on, Neil. Let's get you to the bathroom and I'll check my e-mails later.'

With Neil dressed and sitting in an armchair, and the windows open, Emma was ready to entertain him. A gentle breeze wafted into the room and she was feeling positive about what she could achieve.

'Sudoku, that's what we're going to do this morning. We need to keep our brains active, keep them stimulated, and I can write the numbers.'

She perched on the edge of his armchair and held the book open. She'd suggested he put on some of his usual aftershave as she thought it might make him feel more normal and the scent of citrus made her stomach flip with desire.

'I don't like Sudoku,' he said.

'Let's turn it into a competition.' She hoped that idea might work. 'I've got two books of the puzzles so we can compete against each other. As long as I can be doing an easy one while you do a difficult one.'

'Oh, no, we have to work on the same category and remember I'm at a disadvantage with having to write the numbers with my left hand. I think I should have a couple of minutes' head start.'

'Agreed.' Emma was prepared to give him a head start of an hour if it meant he was engaged with the activity.

By lunchtime they were both flagging.

'I enjoyed our morning together, Emma,' Neil said. 'I think you won, you must have the right mind for it.'

'Well done, me,' she said, happy that the morning had passed in companionship rather than antagonism.

* ★ * ★ *

After lunch Emma could see that Neil was tired and she thought he deserved a rest. After making sure he was comfortable she decided to sort through some of the stuff in the house as she could well not be in the country when it did eventually sell. She would sort out the bits and pieces she wanted to keep and put them in storage, maybe with a few things from her rented flat to clear it a bit for her friend.

She started with a box of mementos stuffed at the back of the wardrobe. There were tickets, programmes, home-made birthday cards from the children and various bits from their wedding.

The decoration from the top of the wedding cake, entwined silver hearts, triggered happy memories and she didn't want to hide it away just yet.

Although she'd barely started her task, she sat on the floor and thought back to the idyllic time when she'd first met Neil, their marriage and then the birth of the children. Such happy times, not always, of course, but compared to how things had crumbled latterly, they had been.

She got up, slipping the wedding topper into her trouser pocket. It was time to get back to the job in hand. There were more mementos from their wedding day than she remembered keeping.

She flicked through the various photos, smiling at images of people who had been guests — her parents, of course, who, although they were very fond of Neil, had never expected Emma to have a shotgun wedding; friends from school and sixth-form college.

Then there was Neil, smiling at her. She was beaming back at him, ecstatic to be his wife and soon-to-be-mother of their child. Who had taken that photo? Emma couldn't remember.

She reached for another piece of paper and her eyes filled with tears as she read the order of service which included their wedding vows. She reached for her handbag and put it into a side pocket. There was no need to tell Neil she'd been going through their past.

After an hour or so, she was pleased with her progress. Her headache was returning. She massaged her temples and decided she'd done enough sorting out for that day.

Poor Neil, having to put up with continual pain. Thinking of him, she wondered again about his bad moods and crankiness. He'd also shown the better side of himself which had resurrected feelings in Emma which she'd thought were long gone, and she was unsettled.

In her bedroom, she opened her laptop and looked on the internet for anything which could give her infor-mation about possible causes for Neil's anxiety, although he had vehemently denied he was anxious. There didn't seem to be anything conclusive. She switched to her e-mails and there was a reply from Neil's firm. Emma went downstairs.

'Neil?'

'What?' he asked, opening his eyes. 'Sorry, Emma, didn't hear you. I've been asleep.'

'Good, best medicine, they say. I just came to let you know your boss has replied to the e-mail I sent on your behalf.'

Neil was immediately more alert.

'I've got the sack, haven't I? What did he say, Emma, come on, just tell me.'

'I'm trying to,' Emma said. 'You've nothing to worry about. He said he was sorry you'd been injured and things would be dealt with in due course, but in the meantime, you were to concentrate on getting better.'

'Phew.' Neil relaxed against his pillow. 'Not sacked, then? Not yet. Wait until they find out it was all my fault.'

'Neil, for goodness' sake, stop being negative. You've been ordered to concentrate on getting better, so why not work towards that? Your first goal is to decide what we're doing this evening.'

'I thought we could do a bit of mountain biking if it won't be too much for you,' he said, smiling at her and getting himself into the upright position.

'I'll try to keep up,' Emma smiled, pleased he was in good humour. 'Last one to the bikes has to get the dinner.'

She watched as Neil tried to launch himself from his bed. He clutched his chest. 'Ouch, that's really painful. Time for painkillers, I think. Can we leave the biking for a few minutes, do you think?'

'I'll get you a drink to swallow the tablets, I'm parched. I've been going through things and there's a fair bit which can go into storage.'

Emma could tell Neil was making a big effort when he didn't refer to the fact that he knew she was preparing things for the move.

'Find anything interesting?' he asked.

Emma didn't tell him about the wedding order of service or the cake topper she'd kept back. She wasn't even sure why she'd done it.

'Just a few things I'd forgotten about.'

A Bit of Pampering

Neil had managed to answer the phone while Emma was in the kitchen. She was pleased he'd made the effort himself rather than calling to her. His lie-in had done him good. She went into the sitting-room with a tray of cereal and tea.

'That was the hospital people,' Neil said. 'They're coming later this morning.' He pulled a face. 'Let's hope they're going to be helpful. I can't see what they can do that you're not already doing, Emma. And I'm sure they don't make as good a cup of tea as you.' He took the drink from her and sipped it.

'I think the idea is that you do these things for yourself, Neil,' Emma said. 'They'll be able to see what needs putting in place to get you back on track. Patience is the key and willingness to do what's advised.'

She was relieved there was some help arriving which would hopefully direct her husband forward. He hadn't made a lot of progress so far, in her opinion.

Emma helped Neil with his washing and shaving ritual after they'd eaten breakfast. Everywhere was clean and tidy and they were ready when the bell rang.

A pleasant and capable-seeming man and his young female assistant came into the room and introduced themselves. The man was Dave and the woman Laura. Neil chatted easily and Emma was pleased that he appeared to have taken to them and didn't view their visit as an intrusion.

'Would you like some tea or coffee?' Neil asked.

'Coffee would be nice,' Dave said.

Emma waited to see what would happen next. Would Neil attempt to put the kettle on, would Dave or Laura encourage him to do so? Or would she be expected to make the coffee?

There was no contest. She went into the kitchen and set out mugs and a plate for biscuits. She heard a movement behind her and turned.

'It's OK, Laura, I can manage,' she said. 'I can make tea and coffee in my sleep. Unlike Neil.'

'I just wanted a word in private, Mrs Cook. Do you have any specific worries?'

'About Neil?' Emma was pleased to have the opportunity of voicing her concerns. 'I was hoping he would be able to do more than he can by now. I have to go abroad soon and I would like to know he can be a bit more independent. Also, I hope you can cheer him up. He seems very miserable.'

'We'll do what we can, but a lot of it will be up to him.'

Emma nodded.

'I'll bring the drinks through. Would you mind taking the biscuits, please?' They returned to the sitting-room.

'I have an appointment in town, so

I'll say cheerio. I hope you get on all right,' Emma said.

'You'll be back for lunch, won't you?' Neil said, sounding anxious.

'I'm not sure. Perhaps Dave and Laura will be able to help you prepare something for yourself,' she said.

★   ★   ★

Emma breathed in the fresh air as she left the house, got into the car and headed towards town.

The beauty salon was just the place she wanted to be. As soon as she walked in, she felt calmer and was looking forward to her time. The receptionist remembered her.

'Mrs Cook, take a seat. Paula won't be long.'

Within a short space of time, Emma was shown into a back room with subdued lighting. The room was partitioned into cubicles giving privacy.

'You've chosen my three favourite things,' Paula confided, 'a massage,

131

manicure and pedicure. Would you like the massage first and then you'll have time to continue relaxing while I do the other treatments?'

'Sounds wonderful.'

'Would you like to choose the colours for your nails?' Paula handed Emma some sample charts and together they selected a soft pink for her manicure and a more daring purple colour for her toenails.

Emma lay face down for her massage and started to relax when soft music filtered into the room. Whatever oils Paula was rubbing gently into her skin smelt divine.

Emma could have fallen asleep, but she had no wish to miss out on this experience. Paula's hands glided over her back and tension melted. All too soon, the treatment was over.

'Lie still for a few minutes and then turn on to your back so I can do your manicure.' Paula's voice was soft and soothing. She was attentive, but not intrusive.

At the end of the session Emma felt as if she'd been on holiday for a fortnight. She didn't want to go straight home, so she walked down to the river and found a café where she ordered a pot of chamomile tea and a chicken satay wrap.

Having grabbed a brief time of respite from looking after Neil, she wanted to make the most of it. She was in no hurry to get home. The river looked silken and cool and she thought how pleasant it would be to kick off her sandals and dangle her feet in the sparkling water.

She remembered the times they'd taken the children to the beach for the day. Ros hadn't been keen on getting her clothes damp if they paddled and a small wave broke as it reached them.

Sam had entertained no such compunction, he'd loved it, reaching down trying to throw some of the water back into the ocean. Neil and Emma had giggled at their antics.

Emma smiled to herself as she

remembered the happy times they'd spent as a family. Not everything had been bad between her and Neil. They'd shared tender, intimate times as well as anger and frustration.

Perhaps it was what every couple experienced. No couple could be completely loved-up all the time. They had been in the beginning, though.

Emma shook her head, wanting to be free from looking back. There was a lot to look forward to now. It was time she went home. She'd played truant long enough.

Emma was relieved to find Neil asleep and so was able to go up to her room and not have to deal with anything potentially confrontational just yet.

Picking up her laptop, she was surprised, but pleased, to find Sam online, so she called him on Skype.

'Hi, Mum. Nice surprise,' Sam said, smiling at her.

'Sam, you're looking tanned and healthy.' Emma smiled back at her son.

'I've just had the most wonderful pampering session, including a massage and look,' she held out her hands, 'I've had my nails painted. I used your birthday gift voucher. It was really great. I've never felt so calm, relaxed and positive as I do at this moment.'

'Glad you're chilled. It's good for you. A bit of spoiling makes you feel good, improves your feeling of self-worth.'

'That's just how I feel. I might have another session at the beauty salon.'

'You should indulge yourself more than you do, Mum. I'm glad I nudged you in that direction. You don't usually do extravagance and luxury. Try to give yourself at least one small daily treat.'

Emma laughed.

'We'll see. I might not have time for that. Dad's home.' She brought Sam up to date with Neil's progress, not putting too much emphasis on the negative side, but telling him Dave and Laura had called to assess him and she was hoping he would improve soon. They

135

talked about what Sam had been up to and where he might go next.

'I've a bit of news about me,' she told him. 'I'm going to Japan.'

'What?' Sam looked startled. 'When? Why? Who with?'

'In a couple of weeks, to teach English as a foreign language, on my own. I think that answers your questions,' Emma said.

'Wow, Mum, that's fantastic. I hope you have an awesome time in Japan, I'm sure you'll love it. I was only there for a short time, but I'd like to go back.

'You mustn't miss going to a tea ceremony and the department stores are worth a visit as they are amazing — they sell everything you can think of all under one roof. Oh, and a trip to the baths is a mind-blowing experience.'

'I'll add them to my list. I'm really looking forward to it.'

'Shame you and Dad can't go together.'

Emma felt uncomfortable. It must be difficult for him to come to terms with his parents separating.

'Ros and I had happy childhoods,' he added, 'and I always thought you and Dad were happy too.'

'We were, some of the time. He was away such a lot, we lost touch with each other, I suppose. We've taken the house off the market as it's a bit much for Dad to cope with at the moment, but it'll be back on soon.'

'I've happy memories of the house, but things change. I'm off to uni when I come home from my gap year, so probably won't be living at home any longer.'

'But you're happy to be travelling still, are you?'

'Oh, yeah, it's great. I love it. Thanks for getting in touch, Mum. We must do this again. Love to Dad.'

Emma blew him a kiss as he disappeared from the screen.

She felt a bit sad about Sam saying he wouldn't be back home to live, but she wouldn't be there anyway.

Another stage in Emma and Neil's

lives was approaching. Things were changing and she accepted that things move on. After all, she was about Sam's age when she was pregnant with Ros.

Going Downhill

After her wonderful day, Emma didn't feel like the mundane task of cooking dinner and she decided quiche, smoked salmon and salad would be easy and quick.

She also decided they would eat at the dining-room table. It was time Neil stopped being such an invalid. She was sure he would feel better once he started getting up and behaving more normally.

'A cold meal?' Neil asked as he sat at the table.

'For three reasons. It's summer, I've cooked you a roast since I've been here, and I didn't feel like spending long in the kitchen this evening. I had a lovely time being pampered this afternoon. Sam gave me a voucher for my birthday. Do you like my nails?' She held them out, just as she had done to show Sam. The response was different.

'You never used to have painted nails. I thought you liked the natural look. I do.'

'I didn't have them done for you, Neil, I had them done for me. I like them.' She watched as Neil shuffled his food round his plate. That wasn't like him. 'Tell me all about your day,' she said.

'What? Being here with those two? They wanted to pry into everything. I felt as though I was being interrogated.' He stabbed at the salmon pieces on his plate and shovelled them into his mouth. Then he sat back in the chair.

'I expect it was just because they want to help you and it's not possible if they don't know anything about you.'

'They know everything about me now.' Neil resumed eating. 'That salmon was quite nice. Is there any more?' he asked.

'Now that's something you could make for yourself. All you need do is open the packet,' Emma said, taking his

140

plate to the kitchen to refill it.

When she returned, Neil was fiddling with the salt and pepper pot.

'I've something to tell you,' he said.

'OK. What sort of something?' Emma was beginning to feel overwhelmed by Neil's unusual behaviour.

'It's serious.' He banged the pepper pot on the table and looked at her.

'Go on.'

'I feel guilty about spoiling your birthday, I'm very sorry about it. You not being able to see your friends because of me and my idiocy.'

'Is that all? Don't worry. It can't be helped. You didn't deliberately crash your car to end up injured. And it was just one birthday. I hope for many more.' She wanted to make him smile, but it seemed there was no chance of that.

'But it was a special birthday. A big one. I didn't get you a card or gift, either. I'll buy you something nice when I can go shopping, although that might be quite a while. Or maybe I'll look on the internet when I feel a bit better.'

'It really doesn't matter.' Emma remembered previous birthday gifts — a vacuum cleaner, a rice cooker and an iron being among them. She didn't want a useful gift from Neil.

Then she remembered the early gifts: pretty earrings, a locket on a chain and a romantic message in a bottle.

'And if you think spoiling my birthday is serious then you don't have too much to worry about.' Emma guessed there must be something else.

'That's not the serious thing I need to tell you.' Neil pushed the food on his plate to one side and put down his fork. 'It's a terrible thing.'

'Go on.'

'I've thought a lot about spoiling your birthday and it's made me feel low and disappointed in myself. But it's not just that. The accident has unnerved me for all sorts of reasons.'

'What sort of reasons?' Emma was sure that talking about his worries would help him.

'It being entirely my fault and thinking how much more serious it could have been. I could have killed someone. A child.'

'But you didn't. There's no point even thinking about that. All you can do is make sure that when you're driving you aren't tired and your mind is on driving, nothing else.'

'Laura and Dave talked to me about my feelings.'

'That's good, isn't it?' Emma asked.

'I don't know.'

'Has it made you feel any better? Any more positive?'

'No. The thing is they said I am suffering from anxiety and depression.'

That explained it.

'What did they say exactly?'

'It's all in those leaflets.' Neil pointed to a small pile of papers at the end of the table. 'But I can tell you pretty much what's in them. There's the shock of the accident, but then feeling afraid afterwards and mood swings, too.' His voice faltered.

'I'm sorry, Emma, I know I've been hard for you to deal with. Laura said the anxiety can cause all sorts of symptoms. Being unable to sleep properly, feeling irritable, having no energy. There's a whole list of things and I don't think I'm suffering from all of them.'

Emma stood and walked round the table to crouch beside his chair. She took his hand.

'At least you're talking. That must be good.'

'Yes, that's what they said. They said talk to family and friends and if that doesn't help, I can get some professional help. It makes me feel awful to be so badly affected. I feel out of control.'

'I understand. I'll read the leaflets, but is there anything else you want to tell me?'

'Returning to a normal routine is one thing which helps, but I obviously can't do that just yet. Eating balanced meals and going for walks are suggested.'

'We could try a short walk tomorrow, if you'd like.'

'Let's see how I feel.'

Emma was devastated by what he'd said even though she'd suspected something of the kind.

'That's fine, Neil,' she said. 'Would you be able to get a better night's sleep if you moved upstairs to the bedroom?'

Neil shook his head.

'It's not that simple — the nightmares will follow me.' He reached out a hand to Emma. 'That's a bit dramatic, isn't it, but it's how I feel. All sorts of nasty thoughts invade my sleep.'

'Things always seem worse at night.'

Emma felt she should offer to sleep in a chair beside him in case he woke in torment, but she didn't want to. He'd managed so far. There must be a simpler solution. She put her hand out for the leaflets.

'Do you mind if I read these tonight?'

'Ideal bedtime reading, I'd say,' Neil said. 'When they discussed the symptoms with me, they were familiar

145

already. I didn't want to admit any of it, though.'

'Why not?' Emma asked. 'You could have told me.'

Neil shook his head and fidgeted in his chair.

'No, you don't understand. It's all a bit unmanly, isn't it? I should have faced up to my problems and dealt with them.' His faced reddened.

'As if they were a work dilemma, you mean?'

'Exactly!'

'Neil, you have to understand that not everything works to a given plan. Our bodies and minds aren't like that. They need a bit more understanding and care.'

They ate their meal at the dining-table and Emma felt that was a step forward — that, and the fact that Neil had felt able to confide in her.

'Would you like coffee now?' she asked, when they'd finished their meal.

'Could we have a walk around the garden first?' Neil said, pushing himself out of his dining chair.

Emma was pleased.

'That would be nice, I'd like that.' She opened the patio doors and they stepped outside. It was a pleasant evening. 'Take care on the uneven slabs. Hang on to me, if you like.' Emma held out an arm which Neil took with his left hand.

'I'll miss you when you've gone, Emma. It's been good to have you around again.'

Emma felt a bit uncomfortable and hoped Neil wasn't going to launch into a 'Please don't go and leave me on my own' speech.

She realised he was feeling unsettled mentally, but her day had been a roller-coaster and she didn't want to deal with Neil's instability at the moment.

'Let's go down and have a look at the apple tree. It's been here longer than we have.'

'The kids used to love to swing from that.'

'I know. It scared the living daylights out of me, but they were always unscathed,' Emma said. 'The garden's a bit untidy, but not too bad.'

'You're thinking about how it will look on a sales brochure, aren't you?'

Emma stopped walking and looked Neil in the eye.

'To be honest, yes, I was, which was silly of me at the moment. I'm sorry.'

Neil shrugged.

'Emma, please don't go away. I'd be lost without you.'

'You've changed your tune. You told me to follow my dream.'

She smiled at her husband to take any sting out of her words as she didn't want to upset him, especially just before he went to sleep.

'I know, I just wish it was nearer home,' Neil whispered, his face close to hers.

Before Emma knew what was happening, she felt his left arm around her and she instinctively slid both her arms around him, feeling his strong body beneath her touch.

Their lips sought each other's and Emma didn't want to pull away from the passionate kiss they shared.

Making the Most
of Each Other

The following day when Emma woke up, she felt a warm glow and then worried. Why ever had she allowed herself to be put in such an awkward situation? Would Neil expect her to end their separation? Had she sent him the wrong signals?

It had been a sudden overpowering feeling, but she wasn't going to let it go any further. She'd have to make sure Neil knew it hadn't meant anything on her part. But was that the truth?

When she entered the kitchen, Neil was already there trying to fill the kettle.

'I thought I'd make tea for a change. I wasn't going to attempt to bring it up to you, but I have been thinking I might move upstairs as you suggested. I'd only need to go up and down once a day.'

Emma was delighted he was more cheerful and moving in the right direction, but worried that telling him nothing had changed regarding their relationship might cause a relapse. She wanted to help him make the tea, but also wanted to avoid any further physical contact if she could.

'Would cereal do for breakfast?' she asked.

'I'll get the packets.'

Emma took bowls from the cupboard and when she stepped back Neil was right behind her and she felt his hand on her shoulder. She turned round.

'Sorry, Neil, I should have looked. I'm not used to you being in the kitchen.'

Neil didn't move.

'I've been a pretty useless husband, haven't I?'

'No, not at all,' Emma said, unable to get out of his way with him in front of her and the kitchen cupboards behind her. Being so close to him, she wasn't sure of her feelings.

She took a deep breath, trying to quell the wave of desire which rose in her. So last night hadn't been a one-off reaction. What was happening?

She could understand that Neil might be infatuated with her and want physical contact, but she should know better and remember she'd moved out of the marital home because they didn't get on. But it seemed they were getting on better now than they had then.

Placing the bowls on the worktop, her hands moved of their own accord towards Neil and caressed his face. She looked deep into his eyes, then kissed his cheek.

When she pulled back, Neil smiled.

'I think a kiss should be on the doctor's prescription instead of those painkillers.'

'Let's have breakfast, shall we?'

There was no denying she was attracted to him and a little spark of love was resurfacing. So much for her good intention of the early morning to keep her distance, but she decided to relax and see how the day went.

'We talked about having a walk today and I'm happy to give it a go, if you don't mind coming with me,' Neil said.

'I'd love to. But we shouldn't go far. I don't want you to tire yourself out.'

'I slept well last night, the first time since the accident. I'm feeling much better today.'

'Please don't get your hopes up, about us. I am going to Japan and I have been building a life of my own.'

'I know, Emma, let's just enjoy this time together.'

That was a better reaction than she'd expected. Maybe talking to her about his anxiety had lifted some of the pressure and it wasn't because he thought there might be a chance of getting back with her. She felt horribly confused, but Neil was right, they should enjoy their time together.

'OK. After breakfast why don't you try to get washed on your own? Then

I'll help you dress. Don't worry about shaving. I don't mind looking at a bit of stubble.'

★ ★ ★

It was cloudy when they left the house, but Neil's smile made it feel sunny to her. It seemed natural to hold hands.

'Do you remember what the chap who married us said about showing your affection in public? We were told to hold hands, put our arms round each other and kiss to show everyone we were in love,' she said.

'And we did.' Neil stopped and put his uninjured arm round her before kissing her. 'There, we've done it again.'

Emma wrapped her arms round his neck.

'Oh, Neil, what went wrong?'

They were interrupted by two teenagers walking past.

'Get a room!' one of them called. Emma and Neil giggled before pulling apart. They decided to go back home.

'The sun's come out so shall we sit in the garden for a bit? We could have lunch outside. I'll get the garden chairs out of the shed,' Emma said.

After settling Neil in the garden, Emma fetched lemonade from the fridge. As she passed the mint growing in the garden she picked a few leaves and added them to the glasses. They sat companionably sipping their drinks, and Emma decided they should talk about how he was feeling.

'So how do you feel today?'

'Good. The walk has made me feel a lot better. And being with you. I know you're going away and I know it may take some time for me to be back to my usual self, but I am starting to feel better.

'Laura and Dave said I'd probably be up and down, but at the moment I think I can manage without professional help. I'd prefer to deal with it all myself.'

'I think we'll have to see how you go. There's no shame in having help. It's not a bad thing.' Emma sat listening to all the sounds. There was a lawnmower in the distance, a bumblebee buzzing in a bush close by and birds singing. And Neil snoring.

Emma took in each detail of his face as he lay asleep. He looked peaceful and happy. If only he could wake and be like that. But she had a feeling his demons would take a while longer to flee from him.

It had been a magical morning, feelings she thought would never have been rekindled appeared instantly, as if they had lain in wait to bind the two of them together again.

It had felt so good to be near Neil, laugh with him, hold hands, hug and kiss — a carefree short time in one morning. Would it vanish when Neil woke up or, worse still, would he think things were now right between them?

Not wanting to tear herself away from watching Neil, Emma sat in her chair and relished her time beside him.

'Hey, you,' Neil said, sleepily moving

his head. 'Are you all right?'

'Fine, just enjoying being lazy.' Emma looked at her watch. 'Shall we have a picnic lunch out here? Sandwiches and so on? I'll go and prepare something and bring out a tray.'

'Can I help?'

'I'll bring out the cutlery and you can lay the table.' Emma went into the kitchen and rooted around in the fridge to see what they could have. She was feeling hungry. Neil still seemed to be in a good mood which was a positive sign. Long may it last.

'This is a feast,' Neil said as Emma brought out a tray laden with food. 'I don't usually eat as much as I have since you've moved back.'

'Glad you're enjoying it,' Emma said. 'I've got into the habit of eating what I like when I like.' She passed the plate to Neil, pleased to see him tucking in. She reached for a ham roll and bit into it. 'We haven't got far with your cookery lessons, have we?'

'No and we probably won't. I hope

Dave and Laura don't push them at me. I couldn't open a tin of soup now.'

'It's difficult with one hand, I'll give you that.' Emma laughed. 'You'll soon be able to manage more easily, it's still early days. How's the pain?'

'Tolerable at the moment.'

When they'd finished eating, Emma took the things back indoors.

'I'm going to attack those weeds and tidy up the garden,' she said, coming back out, dressed in her old clothes. 'Will you stay here or shall I help you inside?'

'I'll stay here. I don't think I can move. Why not join me in being lazy and leave the gardening?' Neil gave her an intimate and affectionate smile.

'I want to be doing something. I'll just potter about.'

Complicated Emotions

Emma found she was taking pleasure in prising out the weeds and neatening the beds. She sat back on her heels and looked up at the house. Unexpectedly, she felt glad the sale had been put off for the time being at least. There was a remote possibility things could work out for them after all.

'Neil, we should both go inside. I don't want Dave or Laura to come and find you ill with sunstroke.'

He struggled out of his chair, refusing her offer of help.

'Delicious as it was, lunch seems an age ago. I'm starving.'

'Me, too, but I'm feeling lazy.'

Neil had a cheeky smile.

'I'll get the dinner,' he said.

'OK, I'll go up and have a leisurely bath while you get on.' She was curious as to what he was up to, but wouldn't be drawn into asking. He obviously had some sort of plan.

It was heaven to sink under the fragrant warm water and relax. Her daily treat, as Sam had instructed her to take. A lot had been accomplished today. She found herself looking forward to spending some more time in Neil's company during the evening.

In clean trousers and top, Emma went downstairs. In the living-room, she sniffed the air.

'No cooking smells. I wonder what you've thought up.'

Neil pulled his left hand from behind his back and held up a leaflet.

'Ta da!'

'Ah, good plan,' Emma said, 'a takeaway.'

'No, it's better than that, home delivery so you don't have to go and collect it. Have a glass of wine while we decide what to order.'

Together they made their selections and Emma reached for the phone. Neil's hand came down lightly on hers.

'No, I said I was in charge of dinner. I'll ring the order through.'

Emma made herself comfortable.

'It looks as if things might be coming together, do you agree? Perhaps the accident was a catalyst for our reunion,' Neil said, while they were waiting for the delivery.

Emma hesitated before replying. They had been good together, but only for a very short time and it might not last. Anyway, she was determined to seize the work opportunity she had been given and wanted. She had been thinking along the same lines as Neil, but was reluctant to voice her thoughts.

'We could sit on the patio to eat if you like. The sun's gone in, but it's still warm,' she said.

'You're changing the subject, Emma. OK, I won't push you. Yes, it will be nice to have another dose of fresh air.'

Emma busied herself setting out the crockery, cutlery and condiments on the patio table.

Neil answered the door when the

delivery arrived and carried the bag through to the patio.

'Chinese meal for two,' he announced.

Emma set out the food on the table. Neil sat next to her so they could both enjoy the view of the garden. As they both reached for plates, their hands touched. It was only a momentary contact, but it was enough for Emma to feel a frisson of desire surge through her.

'It's nice being here with you,' she said. 'I've enjoyed today. It's been relaxing.'

'Like old times?' Neil asked.

Emma considered the question and her answer.

'Not really, but different from how things were during the past few years.'

'I did miss you when you moved out. I know you think I only consider work, but that's not true.'

He leaned towards her. She didn't move away and they shared another loving kiss.

'What I said, about you not going

away, Emma, I shouldn't have said it. Of course you must go,' Neil said, when they pulled away from each other

Emma reached for a spoonful of chicken in black bean sauce.

'I'm definitely going, Neil, but it's good to have your blessing.'

'I'll miss you. And I don't just mean for what you've done around the house. If I hadn't had your company I'd be even more fed up.' Neil made no attempt to help himself to food.

'You'll be OK. I'm sure it's normal after an accident to feel anxious.' Emma didn't know if it was or not, but she didn't want Neil to feel he couldn't cope. 'That's more or less what you were told, wasn't it?'

'That's what I think they meant,' Neil said, putting his good arm around her and pulling her to him again. It was as if they were back in the days when they were in love and couldn't stop themselves being drawn to each other. Their kisses became more intense.

Even though she wanted to have the

physical contact with Neil, Emma extracted herself from his embrace and sat back in her chair.

'This is getting complicated, Neil. I think I'm falling in love with you all over again.'

Neil still held her.

'I may have neglected you, but I never stopped loving you, Emma.'

All Change

'You can't possibly go and leave Dad like this,' Ros said. 'Look at him, he can hardly cope with anything and he's had to sleep downstairs. No wonder he can't get a good night's rest.'

Emma tried to explain that Neil was improving, his pain was slowly lessening and he planned to sleep upstairs soon, but Ros wasn't listening.

Ros went over to Neil.

'Poor Dad,' she said, kissing his cheek and throwing her arms around him, hugging him tightly.

'Ow, watch it, Ros, I'm still a bit tender.' Neil gasped and tottered into the chair behind him.

'See, Mum, he needs full-time care. He's in such pain.'

'I wouldn't have been if you hadn't squeezed me so hard, Ros. But it was nice to have a hug. Now, let's be clear about your mother going away. She gave up her dream once and she's not going to have to do it again if I've got anything to do with it.'

'But it's not fair on you, Dad. What will you do?' Ros was near tears.

'It's all right, sweetheart, Dave and Laura will look in on me, I can manage to wash more or less on my own. I'm not doing too badly.'

'But what about your meals?'

'I'll manage,' Neil said. 'Someone has been looking in on me from the rehab team and they know Mum's going away.'

'Shall I make some tea?' Emma offered.

'I'll help,' Ros said, following her mum to the kitchen.

'I'm sorry you're upset, Ros,' Emma said, 'but you both knew I had plans to go away. I looked after your dad as well as I could for as long as I could.'

Emma wasn't sure why she felt she should explain to Ros. Her daughter was already aware of the situation and hadn't visited Neil as often as she might have done since the accident almost three weeks ago.

'I know, Mum, it's just that I hadn't realised he'd be as weak and frail as he is. Dad's never ill.'

'He'll get better, Ros. It's just a question of time.'

Emma put teabags into three mugs and poured on hot water.

'I'll come and live here when you go,' Ros said unexpectedly. 'I mean it, Mum. I haven't exactly been the devoted daughter, have I? It's the work thing I've been sweating over. But I suppose I can sweat as much here as at my flat.'

★   ★   ★

Emma couldn't believe how quickly the three weeks she'd spent with Neil had gone. Nor could she believe how strongly she felt for him.

As she finished packing the last bits

and pieces in her luggage, she wondered if she was doing the right thing. I'll only be away a year, she told herself. If she still felt the same for Neil when she returned they could take their time and see how their relationship developed.

When she went downstairs she found Neil and Ros in the sitting-room chatting about work.

'Sorry to interrupt, but my taxi will be here soon, so I'd better say goodbye. Let's not prolong our farewell, as it will make me sad.'

'You're regretting going, Mum?'

'No, but I'll be unhappy not to see you for a whole year. Maybe you could visit.'

'It depends on work. At the moment none of us can take any leave.'

Emma looked at Neil who raised his eyebrows and smiled. He pushed himself to standing and walked over to her.

'I'm going to miss you.' He took her hand. 'Keep in touch. You'll have a great time, I'm certain.'

'Take care, Neil, and make sure you ask for help if you feel you need it. Ros will make sure you're OK, won't you?'

'Of course, you don't need to worry about Dad. I'll work from home some days and when I do go in I'll have my phone with me all the time and be ready to come back if he needs me. Although I am a bit worried about work.'

'There's no need to be,' Neil said. 'I'll be fine on my own and will enjoy hearing all about your project when you come home in the evenings. It will be good to have you living at home again.'

The sound of a car horn alerted them to the taxi's arrival.

'Here goes,' Emma said, before kissing them both. As her lips brushed Neil's cheek, she had the urge to prolong her contact with him, but with Ros around, it would be awkward. It seemed Neil might share her views as his left hand tightened on her arm as if wanting to remain connected with her.

'Good luck, Mum, enjoy yourself.'

'Yes, good luck, enjoy yourself and come back,' Neil added.

'I'm definitely coming back.' Emma walked into the hall and trundled her luggage out to the waiting car. Once seated in the taxi, she looked towards the family home and waved at the two figures standing outside the front door. She took a deep breath.

'Terminal three, Heathrow, please.'

★   ★   ★

Emma had always felt a sense of excitement when they'd travelled by plane for family holidays in other countries. And even the long queue for security didn't dampen her feelings. She had no idea what living on her own in a strange country would be like.

Then she thought of Sam who was travelling the world and taking it all in his stride. If her eighteen-year-old son could do that then she was sure she could manage a year in a much more structured stay.

Settled in her seat on the plane with her seat belt buckled ready for take-off, Emma looked around. She'd been lucky to get a window seat and in the seats next to her were a man and woman, much the same age as herself she guessed, who were clearly in a loving relationship.

They weren't speaking English so she couldn't eavesdrop, but they made each other laugh and were physically close. They touched each other and held hands, and often kissed. Emma wondered about their relationship. Was it new or had they been together a long time?

She also wondered how she and Neil would be behaving if they were together on the plane. Outward displays of intimacy between them had become few and far between over the years.

As the plane taxied to the runway, Emma's excitement mounted. At last she was on the way to her big adventure. But sadness wormed its way into her heart as she thought of Neil.

After the past few weeks she no longer knew if she'd made the right decision when she'd left him and lived on her own. As the plane took off her stomach lurched. Was she making the right decision to live in Japan away from everyone and everything she knew?

Yes, she decided, but she wished Neil was sharing the experience.

The Adventure Begins

Emma was feeling a little jaded after the 14-hour flight. They'd been well looked after and she'd enjoyed the meals and in-flight entertainment.

The wait for the luggage to appear on the carousel seemed to take for ever, and she was pleased when she walked through into the arrivals hall and saw her name on display amongst the crowd of waiting people. She made her way towards the woman holding the sign.

'Hello, I'm Emma Cook.'

'Hello, *yokoso*, welcome. I am Hanami, I work at the language school in the office. I hope you will enjoy your stay here. We will go to my car, then I will take you to your apartment. It is close to the school and I have visited it to make sure it is all right for you.'

'Thank you.'

Emma tried to take in the journey from the airport to her new home, but fatigue overcame her and the surroundings blurred. Hanami pointed out various landmarks and was attentive. Then the car pulled up alongside a drab building.

'Here we are at your place,' Hanami said, gesturing towards a drab-looking building.

Although Emma hadn't been expecting a palace, she was a little disappointed by what she saw. The inside might well be totally different, she told herself.

'It is on the second floor and you will find it quite basic.'

'I'm sure it will be fine,' Emma said. The school had found the apartment for her as it was difficult for foreigners to negotiate accommodation, but it was subsidised, which was helpful.

At the door, Hanami handed Emma a key.

'You unlock your new room,' she said.

Emma did, and was surprised at the

bareness and smallness of it.

'We have fitted some things in for you, Mrs Cook.'

Emma supposed she meant the small TV, single gas hob and fridge, which made a whirring noise. The futon didn't come as a big surprise and she hoped it was comfortable.

'Oh, a balcony,' she said. 'That's nice.'

'Useful for airing and drying clothes,' Hanami said. 'Unless it is wet and cold outside. In that box,' Hanami nodded towards a corner of the room, 'there are a few basic food items. I will go now, Mrs Cook, unless you have any further need of me.'

'Please call me Emma. And where and when should I go to start work?'

Hanami handed her a folder.

'All the details are in here. Contact numbers and so on. I've included a map of the area as well, showing a local shop where you can get whatever you need. And my mobile phone number is there also. Please call me if you have any problems at all. I am delighted to help you. You can rest, you come to the college tomorrow. Goodbye for now, Emma.'

Left on her own, Emma sprawled on the futon, thinking she hadn't slept that near the floor for a very long time.

Her luggage filled most of the unoccupied space and she wished she hadn't brought as much. She would have to get it put away and stack the cases somewhere.

Opening the folder which Hanami had given her, she looked at her schedule for the following day. She was to be at the college by midday. Not an early start, thank goodness.

Hanami had also included useful information such as a taxi phone number, which Emma decided she would call to get her to the college for her first day at work. She felt excited and a little daunted.

After flicking through the folder she'd been given, Emma got up and walked around the tiny space which would be her home for the next twelve months.

She opened a door and found the toilet, basin and shower. How she would manage in so small an area, she had no idea. It was smaller than the wardrobe in the spare room at home.

Home! She'd have to let Neil and Ros know she'd arrived safely. Unable to keep her eyes open any longer, she lay down and went to sleep, after setting the alarm on her phone so she wouldn't be late getting up.

⋆　⋆　⋆

When she woke, it took Emma a few moments to realise where she was. She made some tea and took it back to bed. She'd give herself ten minutes before getting up and sorting her things.

There was a small cupboard and a chest of drawers her clothes and other bits and pieces would fit in.

The apartment was painted white and looked cold and bare, but it was clean and functional. It seemed to have everything she would need. A table in the corner could be used for eating and working.

She looked up and out of the window. The view was of other apartment blocks. It was a bit different to her spacious house and views of the garden at home. Her home, she reminded herself, could well be on the market in a few months. Resisting the urge to contact Neil, she finished her drink and got up.

By eleven she had finished her unpacking and had her bag ready with everything she would need for the afternoon. She had just one lesson of 90 minutes scheduled and was confident one of the lesson plans she'd brought with her would work with the small group of people she would be teaching.

The information folder she had been given was comprehensive and she flicked through it again as she forced down a dry roll with some coffee.

Already the apartment, which was smaller than it had looked in the photos, seemed more homely with her bits and pieces dotted around. But apprehension overcame her at the thought of meeting her students, and her first lesson.

Before phoning the taxi firm she crossed her fingers that the person who answered would speak English, otherwise she would be completely stuck.

A Warm Welcome

She was relieved to see Hanami sitting at the reception desk when she arrived at the language school. On seeing Emma she immediately stood up and walked round to greet her.

'Emma, how was your first night in Japan?'

'Good, thanks, I slept well and now I'm ready to start work.'

'Your class is at two. Come into the office and meet the team.'

After being introduced to the office staff who were all very friendly and welcoming, Hanami invited her to sit with her in reception.

'You have been given groups of older people to teach. They mostly have some English, but want to become more fluent. The information I gave you should have given you some idea of their level, but it may take a few lessons until you get it quite right for them. Someone will come and watch one of your lessons later on. Not to criticise, but to help.'

'OK, thanks.' Emma didn't mind people sitting in with her — she knew it would be helpful.

'Although you will be teaching older groups conversational English, we understand you may want to work with young people sometimes. I can timetable an occasional session with youngsters. Just let me know.'

'I will. Your English is excellent, Hanami.'

'I lived and studied in England for a year. I will tell you all about my stay, but not now. We often go out together for meals or to the cinema and we can talk then, if you would like to join us.'

'I'd love to, thank you.' Emma was pleased to find she'd already made at least one friend in Japan.

'Now I will take you to the room where your first session will be. There will be eight people in the group, if they

181

all turn up. I will leave you to prepare. Would you like a drink?'

'No, thanks, I have a bottle of water.'

Emma followed Hanami to a small classroom. As she sat there going over her notes again, she felt she should pinch herself to make sure she wasn't dreaming. At last she was about to teach.

⋆ ⋆ ⋆

Emma felt like skipping back to her apartment. Her first group of students had been attentive and keen to learn. They had also been very welcoming and friendly.

Her plan now was to call in at the supermarket on her way home and then to spend the evening preparing lessons for the next day, as well as contacting Neil, Ros and Sam.

The supermarket looked at first glance pretty much like one at home apart from the signs which were of no use to her at all. Once she started looking at the shelves and displays she found all sorts of things she wanted to try.

There was a large fish and seafood section and a huge selection of rice brands. She picked up some dried seaweed and a packet of rice. Then she spotted some ready-made dishes and chose fried chicken, croquettes and sautéed vegetables. She would try and remember their Japanese names, *korokke* and *kinpira*.

It was exciting to be having new experiences and she looked forward to telling her family all about it.

★　★　★

The days at the college were wonderful as far as Emma was concerned. She loved imparting information to the students in a way they could understand, and found herself almost overrunning on time as she and the group warmed to their subject. The students couldn't have been nicer, Emma told herself. They were polite, agreeable and eager to learn.

By her second session with them on Friday, she felt she'd known the original group for ages.

'I look forward to seeing you next week,' she said. A hand went into the air. 'Yes, Gaku?'

'We and Hanami would like to take you for some tea,' Gaku said.

Emma was touched.

'That is very kind,' she said. 'When shall we go?'

'Now,' the group chanted.

Laughing, Emma followed them out of the college and they ambled along back streets until Gaku stopped.

'Here,' he said, opening the door for her.

The café was stark and bare, but clean and there were several customers.

'Please sit,' Gaku said. 'Aimi and me will get tea.'

When the tea was poured, Emma raised a cup to her mouth. Before sipping, she inhaled.

'Gaku, this is cherry tea, isn't it?'

Gaku and the group grinned.

'Sencha tea, cherry and rose. We like it.'

'I like it, too, and I like being here with you.'

'I like English tea,' Hanami said.

'Of course, you told me you'd spent a year in England. Where did you study?' Emma asked.

'A language school in Cambridge. I lived with a family and their two children. I had a good opportunity to practise my English and I sampled many British dishes — shepherd's pie, roast dinner, apple pie, summer pudding, toad in the hole . . .'

'What is that?' Gaku interrupted. 'I thought a toad is an animal. How do you eat it in a hole?'

Emma thought that in her classes she should be aware how her words could be taken literally and misunderstood.

'It is sausages cooked in a batter — a bit like tempura. It was good.'

'Did you get the chance to see much

of the surrounding area when you were there?' Emma asked.

'The school organised outings and also my family took me places at weekends. We went punting, to the seaside, and also went to London and saw the sights and went to the theatre. Shakespeare was very difficult to understand.

'I was also taken to my host family's friends' houses and saw how they lived and their different interests. It was fascinating.'

Emma wondered about Hanami's family and how she could afford a year's language school. She didn't like to ask, but was dying to know.

'That must have cost a lot of yen, Hanami, how could you afford that?' Aimi asked.

Emma was pleased Aimi had asked the question she wanted to know the answer to.

'My family in Japan want me to speak excellent English, so my grand-mother bequeathed me enough money to take a trip to the UK. I promised I'd do the very best I could.' She took a sip of tea. 'I find I am still learning. Words are fascinating, along with their origins.'

Emma couldn't agree more.

'How wonderful to be given an opportunity like that. Your family have every reason to be proud of you, Hanami.'

'I hope so. And I will visit my English family again, but there's been enough talking about me,' Hanami said. 'It's someone else's turn now.'

They sat and chatted for almost an hour until Aimi said she had to go as she was looking after her grandchildren that evening. After they'd left, Emma found herself wondering about her students' lives. They were probably wondering about hers. She gathered her things and left the café, promising herself she would return as it was such a friendly place.

Handsome Stranger

On Saturday, the sound of birdsong woke Emma from a deep and dreamless sleep. She stretched out on her mattress and thought briefly about staying there for the day. What a waste of time that would be. Sightseeing had to be the order of the day.

She grabbed the map and her tourist book from her bag and studied them before making tea and wondering what to have for breakfast. Fish with rice and pickles sounded interesting, but she'd have to go out and have that and she felt she needed to fuel up before her tour of the area. Fruit and yogurt were in the fridge, so they would do.

The trips to the art galleries, museums and shops were splendid and Emma only made short tours of them, promising herself she'd come back later and do them in detail. Perhaps she could bring the students here and they could teach each other things; she had a feeling they'd enjoy that.

By late afternoon, she was tired, hungry and thirsty. She decided to go to the café where she'd been with the students the afternoon before. Proud of herself for having negotiated the twisting back streets, Emma ordered a melon soda.

The café was crowded, but she saw a couple leaving and took their table. The soda was delicious and refreshing. Emma was debating whether to order something to eat, when she was aware of someone standing next to her. She looked up.

'Mind if I join you?' the stranger asked. 'Not much room, is there?' He smiled and waited for her to answer.

'Of course, please sit down.' He was one of the few Westerners Emma had been close to all week. She studied him, taking in his craggy face. He was handsome but although he was probably still in his forties, his hair was flecked with grey.

'Thanks. That looks interesting,' he said, nodding towards Emma's drink.

'Melon soda,' Emma said, 'plus a blob of ice-cream.'

'I've ordered boring coffee, but then I am American.'

'So I gathered.'

'Ah, the accent, sure thing.' He laughed and Emma suddenly felt pleased he'd asked to share her table.

★　★　★

Emma led her small group through the museum, knowing they were enjoying it.

'Have you been here before?' she asked.

'Before? We have been here?' Aimi sounded puzzled and Emma found an opportunity for a short lesson.

They stopped in a corner.

'‘Before’ means at an earlier time,' Emma explained. 'I said ‘before’ meaning have you ever been here.' Their puzzled faces told her she hadn't explained it well. 'I expect it was my mistake,' she said. 'I should just have asked if you have visited this museum.'

They relaxed and smiled at one another using words Emma didn't understand.

'No, we have not been here before.'

'Very good. Excellent,' Emma said. She was about to move them on to another exhibit when she was sure she saw the American from the café. He was slouching against a pillar looking at a leaflet. 'Would you excuse me, please?' she said to the group.

'Hi,' Emma said.

The American looked up and smiled at her.

'Hi yourself. How are you?'

'Very well,' Emma said.

'I'm pleased you're immersing your-self in cultural things as well as sodas.'

'That's my group,' Emma said. 'I'm a teacher.' She was proud to say that.

'Pity,' the American said. 'I would

have liked to invite you for a drink or something.'

'That sounds good. I'll be free later.' Emma Cook, what are you doing, she asked herself. Flirting and being forward, that's what. She found she didn't care.

'Great, where shall we meet and at what time?' They negotiated time and place and Emma went back to the group.

★　★　★

'*Matane*, see you soon,' Emma said when they'd finished their visit to the museum. What an amazing day! She'd had a fantastic time with the Japanese students and now she was meeting the enigmatic American.

She almost flew to their rendezvous, wishing she'd had time to go home for a shower and change of clothes. It's only a cup of coffee, she told herself, calm down.

'I've saved you a seat.' He smiled as

she entered the café, stood up and held out his hand. 'I'm Logan.'

Emma put her hand in his and he clasped it firmly.

'I'm Emma.'

'Pretty name. What will you have?'

Emma was hungry. She hadn't eaten lunch as she'd been too busy preparing the outing with her students.

'May I have something to eat, please?'

'Sure, have what you like. I'm having some sushi, want some?'

'Yes, please.'

Logan came back with a tray of food and some glasses. He unloaded them on the table.

'Sushi, sashimi and sake.'

Emma was about to protest about the sake, but could find no reason to. Her responsibilities for the day were over, the time was her own now. She'd had sushi, but never sashimi, and was a bit hesitant. Hunger overcame her and she took some of each, savouring the difference and screwing up her face at the acidity of the daikon.

'What's the verdict?' Logan said.

'Delicious. I'd definitely have it again.'

'Let's hope that's with me. Shall we have another glass of sake?'

They had a good time chatting and laughing. Emma found Logan excellent company and he was considerate and polite towards her. Fleetingly she thought of Neil, but she was here and he was in England, so she pushed the thoughts aside and enjoyed Logan's flattery and company.

Fun with Friends

A few days later after the morning session, the students had a discussion in Japanese while Emma was putting her laptop in her bag.

'Emma,' Aimi said, 'we would like to go out this afternoon rather than stay in class. We will talk English all the time and will learn.'

'Where would you like to go? The art gallery next to the museum looks as though it might be interesting.'

'We would like you to have a Japan . . . um, I don't know how you say it.'

'I think you say a Japanese experience,' Gaku said.

'That's very good and I'd love to try it, whatever it is.' Emma wondered what she was letting herself in for.

They all laughed.

'It is to go to a Sento.'

'A Sento?' Emma was sure she'd read

the word, but couldn't now remember what it was.

'A bath for everyone,' Aimi said. 'When we have bathed, we can sit in the garden. You will like that.'

Emma had seen pictures of the pretty tranquil gardens at these places. They often had a pool. She was pleased there would be an opportunity to visit the Sento and its garden.

'A communal bath house. It would be wonderful to go with you.' Emma had read about them and Sam had said it was mind-blowing. She was delighted to be going with her students. She'd thought about going on her own, but not knowing the etiquette she'd been worried she might offend someone.

The entrance to the building looked a little like a temple. After they'd paid, they all took off their shoes and put them in lockers. Then the men in the group went one way and Emma followed the women the other way through an entrance curtain to a changing room with more lockers.

'I bought these for you.' Aimi handed her a towel, a smaller towel and some toiletries. 'The people here will help you with anything.'

'Attendants would be a good word to use,' Emma said.

'Come.' Aimi opened a sliding door. 'We go through here and wash first.'

The next room had a huge painting of Mount Fuji on the wall at the far end. The room had mirrors along two of the walls. Under each mirror was a shelf with a wooden bucket, two taps and a shower head.

'We sit on a stool and wash.' Aimi sat on one of the stools and indicated for Emma to sit at the stool next to her. 'We must get clean and then get all the soap off.'

Emma followed her lead and started by rinsing herself before washing with soap and rinsing again. She knew entering the large baths with soap on her body would be frowned upon so she rinsed herself again.

'Ready?' one of the women asked.

'Yes.' Emma followed the others to the large steaming baths at the end of the room and got in slowly.

'*Gokuraku, gokuraku*,' Aimi said. 'It feels good?'

'Wonderful.' Emma closed her eyes and let her body slide into the water.

'They are different heats. You can try another hotter bath later. Some baths use natural hot water, but not this one,' Megu told her.

As Emma luxuriated in the bath and listened to the women chatting, she had to agree with Sam that this was an incredible custom. She'd read that some people thought bathing not only washed away physical dirt, but spiritual grime too. She could well believe it.

Feeling refreshed from her unexpected and marvellous Japanese experience of the previous day, Emma found she had more things to look forward to.

Logan had texted to arrange a meeting and she'd accepted. There were some supplies she wanted and she thought the department store would be just the place to go. Sam had mentioned they sold everything, so she was going to put it to the test.

Logan was waiting for her outside the store. She took a few minutes to look at him without being observed. They'd met a few times since their sushi and sashimi meal and Emma had loved being with him. He made her laugh, complimented her and was generally good company. As if he sensed her presence, he looked up, grinned at her and waved.

'Hi,' Logan said, stepping towards her.

'You don't mind shopping, do you?' Emma remembered Neil had hated it, unless it was something he needed for work or a part for his bike.

Logan shrugged.

'Why should I? I'm in Japan with a beautiful woman, what more can I ask for?' He smiled at her. 'To answer your question, no I don't mind at all. I'm looking forward to it.'

The store was a revelation. She'd

only skimmed the surface when she had been before, but now she was determined to investigate it thoroughly.

As Sam had said, there seemed to be no end to what you could buy, from a tin of beans to a fancy-dress costume. This was a serious shopping sensation. She could bring the students here.

Then she dismissed the students from her mind and concentrated on being with Logan.

Laden with bags of clothes and a few delicacies Emma couldn't pronounce, she flagged.

'I think I've had enough shopping for one day. I'll definitely come back. Wow, what a fabulous experience. Thanks, Logan. Where to now?'

'A sit down, I think. I know a place nearby.'

The tea house was enchanting and they sat in the garden.

'I enjoy being with you, Emma. It's fun looking around places, but it's quite lonely being single.'

Emma realised she knew next to

nothing about Logan.

'Have you ever been married?'

He pulled at his collar.

'I've been married twice, once when I was twenty-three and in lust rather than in love. Kelly hated that I strayed and walked out after two years.

'When I was thirty I met a kind, gentle woman, Gracie, who maintained her independence and was a free spirit. We'd been together for twelve years before she passed over after two years of agonising suffering and pain. We had no children, were content with each other.

'Home is empty now,' he continued, 'and I want to go to other places to immerse myself in something different. After she died, I really wanted to make enough money to get away from home as it reminded me too much of Gracie.'

Emma was appalled that she'd made him relive his grief.

'I'm really sorry, Logan. It must have been a dreadful time. I'm glad you found true love with Gracie.'

He smiled, but his eyes were sad.

'I was blessed.' He cleared his throat. 'I've seen a lot of the world and am now interested in foreign places, people and their culture. I like to have a bit of luxury, however, and don't stint myself on accommodation, travel options and so on. I like to go first class.'

'I'm sure I'd like it, too, but the college doesn't pay that well,' Emma said.

'I was a realtor and I made good money on properties and then I started flipping houses which made me rich enough to retire,' Logan explained.

Emma raised her eyebrows.

'Flipping?'

'Guess it's an American word. It's buying houses at knock-down prices, doing them up and selling them on at a profit.' They sat for a while then Logan leaned towards her. 'Are you hungry? I fancy a cheese roll, want to join me?'

Emma was starving, but in Japan the last thing she wanted to eat was a cheese roll and was puzzled as to why he was offering it. Not wanting to offend him, she nodded her head.

Logan went off to the counter and came back with a loaded tray.

'One cheese roll,' he said, handing her a plate.

'This isn't a cheese roll,' Emma said. To her it looked like a green Arctic roll ice-cream.

'It's a green tea sponge spread with a mixture of cheese, like mascarpone I guess, and cream and rolled up,' Logan said. 'And I got green tea as I like the natty bamboo handles on the pots.'

'It's totally awesome,' Emma declared.

After a short detour to drop off Emma's purchases at her apartment, the two of them decided to spend the rest of the day together.

They walked for miles, chatting and pointing out things to each other. Although Logan had no children, he was interested in hearing about Ros and Sam. Emma was reluctant to talk about Neil and Logan didn't ask.

They stopped for noodles at a bar.

'I'm making a mess,' Emma spluttered, wiping her chin.

'Missed a bit.' Logan took a serviette and dabbed her cheek, his eyes twinkling as he did so. 'I'll take you out for more noodles if I get to do this each time.'

'No need, I'll brush up on my technique.' Emma enjoyed his attention.

'Are you happy to carry on sightseeing when we've finished here?'

'I'd love to. It's great looking at things with you. I'm loving it,' Emma said, putting her hand on his. She knew she was flirting. It had been a long time since she had flirted with anyone. It felt good.

★   ★   ★

When Logan saw Emma home later that evening, he didn't come into the apartment but gave her a soft kiss on her cheek.

'See you soon, sweetheart. It's been a

good day for me, and for you, I hope.'

Emma squeezed his hand.

'It's been great.'

She had enjoyed the day and Logan's company. Behind her closed door, she examined her feelings in private. She was very fond of Logan, but he was nothing like Neil.

Unexpected tears pricked her eyes as she remembered their dating days and the times in their marriage when they'd been close.

Going to the small safe in a cupboard, she opened it and retrieved the marriage vows she'd brought with her from England. At the time, it had been an instinctive reaction, probably just to keep the thought of Neil close to her, but now she read them and went to bed that night thinking about them.

News from Home

Emma had been madly busy with work and social life and had only briefly communicated with Neil and Ros. The reception on her phone was rubbish at times and she wondered if her e-mails were getting through.

She missed Neil and Ros and the first thing she wanted to do was chat to Neil, but with the time difference, would have to wait until later in the day. She sent a text for him to pick up when he woke.

As she did her washing and tidied the flat she thought of Neil. He had been on her mind a lot over the past few weeks and she longed to know how he was getting on.

Ros had sent her very short messages saying everything was OK, but had given no details. Emma wondered if Ros had been neglecting her dad, not through unkindness, but just because she was too busy.

Emma had kept this Sunday free to give herself a chance to catch up with domestic tasks and admin. In the middle of hanging her washing out on the balcony she paused and stood to take in her surroundings.

Depression wasn't something she knew much about, but she was sure it wouldn't disappear in a few weeks. She needed to know Neil was coping.

Somehow the day dragged, but finally it was nearing the time she had suggested. Sitting at her computer she waited to see if Neil would call her and a few minutes later she heard the ringtone and quickly accepted the video call.

It took a few seconds for Neil's face to appear on the screen. She felt excited to see him, but was shocked that he had lost weight. Maybe it was simply distortion of the image, she thought.

'Neil, how are you?'

'OK. You?'

'Good, thanks. I'll tell you more about my time here, but first I want to know everything about you and how you are doing.'

Neil didn't say anything. Emma was worried by his lack of response.

'How are you getting on, Neil?'

'I think I'm doing OK. I've been to a couple of the meetings of the support group Laura suggested and gave me . . . '

'Sorry, Neil, you keep breaking up. What did you say?'

The connection was broken. She called him and they were reconnected much to her relief.

'Hello. It's amazing we can see each other to talk when we're all those miles apart, but still frustrating when it doesn't work. What were you saying? Something about the support Laura suggested and gave you?' Emma asked.

'Oh, gave me details for.'

'How did it go?'

'Fine. There were some interesting people there.'

Emma was worried he still seemed

very low. He didn't maintain eye contact with her and seemed preoccupied. She would do her best to be upbeat and cheer him up.

'I'm guessing Ros isn't cooking you gourmet dinners,' she said.

He smiled.

'Hardly. It's usually a microwave meal when it's her turn, but I've cooked a few nice meals. Proper ones like you'd do. I haven't done a roast yet. I'm working up to it. Ros has helped with the things I couldn't manage to do.'

'That's great. And you're getting out and going for walks?'

'Every day. My ribs don't hurt very much now and my arm feels a lot better so things are looking up in that respect. I miss you, though. With not working I've had a lot of time to think about you, about us. How we used to be in the early days. I feel sad that I made you unhappy and we separated.'

Emma felt torn. Those few weeks they'd spent together had shown her she still had strong feelings for Neil and yet she'd let herself be ensnared by Logan's kindness and charm. She really didn't want to talk to Neil about her feelings as she was on an emotional roller-coaster.

'I must show you my flat. It will only take a couple of minutes. It's tiny. The shower room is the size of one of our wardrobes. Look, this is where I eat and do my work. There's my futon. The kitchen area is here and now I'll show you the bathroom.'

As she walked, she panned her laptop round so he could see everything she was talking about.

'It's minute compared to our spacious home, isn't it?'

'You still call it home, Emma.'

Emma was uneasy when he noticed that, but quickly recovered.

'It's been my home for a long time.' Then she sat down and told him some amusing stories about what she'd been teaching the students, and how amenable they were.

'I've been to a communal bath.'

210

'Have you made any friends?'

She wouldn't mention Logan.

'Some of my students have become friends. They took me to the baths and out for tea and we've been to a museum together.'

'I'm glad for you.'

As she glanced at him, Emma could tell he didn't look very pleased. It seemed to be like pulling teeth trying to get him to open up and be a little positive. She tried another tack.

'Tell me about the group you've been to. You said you met interesting people. Did it help talking to them?'

At last there seemed a flicker of interest in his eyes.

'I think so. It's amazing how differently people live their lives. There was I, thinking it was all down to money and succeeding in one's job but I've met some people who don't have a job or even an income except benefits. I'm learning a lot. In fact, Emma, I must tell you . . . '

The connection was lost and she was

cut off from him once more. She tried again, but with no luck.

Emma spent a restless few hours wondering what Neil had been going to tell her. She couldn't settle in the now oppressive apartment, so went out for a walk, trying to weigh up the pros and cons of the tête-à-tête she'd had with him.

On the positive side, he had got in touch with her, even if it had been at her instigation, and had opened up a little about what was going on at home.

She didn't think he had deliberately ended the call as she knew from her own experience that the internet didn't always function well. Also, on the positive side, Neil had said he was following up something Laura had suggested to him, but hadn't said much about it, probably due to the fact that they'd been cut off.

On the negative side, he'd looked dreadful — drawn and pale, he'd lost weight and didn't seem happy. He might have been pretending to be positive about the group he'd been to so Emma wouldn't guess something was wrong.

Emma had little experience of mental illness, so didn't know if that was what still troubled Neil. She knew depression could be a difficult challenge. When she'd been through dark situations when Neil had been absent, she'd known dreadful days when she'd been in the doldrums, but it wasn't a depression like Neil was facing.

She stopped to cross a road, unaware of where she was. There was a garden on the opposite side of the street and she decided to go there. She'd read about *shinrin-yoku*, forest bathing, and had briefly discussed it with her students one afternoon.

It hadn't been something she'd contemplated before, but as it basically meant walking through forested areas, maybe she could improvise in the garden. It was meant to reduce stress and Emma needed that now. Perhaps it might be something she could pass on to Neil — if she ever managed to get in touch with him again.

After half an hour of trying to slow down and calm herself, Emma decided she had to put her worries about Neil aside and concentrate on her new life.

Turning back the way she'd come, Emma hoped she'd find her way home. Usually, she was in the habit of carrying the very useful map of the area with her, but she'd come out without giving it a thought.

She could always practise her Japanese by asking the way. The thought made her smile as she hadn't been concentrating on Japanese words at all. Maybe that should be her homework and she could surprise her students the following week.

Coming to Japan had been a momentous decision and she didn't regret it at all, although there was a tiny niggle still about Neil.

Her feelings for him had grown rather than diminished and she would have liked to share her adventures with him.

The culture, people and almost everything else was thought-provoking and she felt sure that when she did eventually go home, she would take a part of Japan in her heart.

Wrong Impression

The tiny niggle which had disturbed Emma's thoughts earlier didn't go away. In fact it grew. Emma knew she would have to try to get back in touch with Neil.

She set up the video call and waited. There was no answer, so she tried Ros who answered.

'Hi, darling, it's Mum. You look well. Are you OK?'

A smiling Ros beamed at her.

'Hi yourself. I'm fine. Working hard, looking after Dad, you know.'

'That's why I've got in touch, Ros. I don't know if you are aware we were skyping earlier on, but the connection went. Just cut out.'

'Yeah, Dad said something about that. Is that why you're getting back in touch? To speak to him?'

'Not that it's not good to be speaking to you.'

'It's OK, I understand. Dad's asleep at the moment.'

'And you're coping with him?' Emma said, exchanging smiles with her daughter.

'Just about.'

'So your dad's getting on all right, is he?'

Ros considered.

'Physically he's doing OK, I'd say — and Laura's always saying he's getting on well. But he often seems down, low, you know.'

'Depressed?' Emma said.

Ros nodded.

'I've tried to occupy him with games of chess and Scrabble. I'm doing my best. I either work from home or leave him for short periods. I don't want him to think I'm babysitting him, but neither do I want to neglect him.'

'Ros, I'm sure you'd never neglect him. You're doing a really good job. But depression is difficult to gauge.'

'That's what Laura said. He's going to a group, but he hasn't said a lot about it. I'm taking it as a good sign that he's been more than a couple of times and is always ready when the taxi comes to pick him up.'

There was an awkward silence as Emma debated asking Ros more about Neil's mood. A knock at the door interrupted her thoughts.

'I'll have to get that, Ros. Sorry.' Emma opened the door to Logan, who came into the flat before she'd had the chance to tell him she was busy. Deciding that she should introduce him to Ros, she beckoned him over to the screen and introduced him as one of her friends.

'Hi, Ros,' Logan said, waving at her. 'I've brought your mom some flowers. I'll go get a vase.' He went straight to the bottom of her clothes cupboard, making it obvious he knew his way around her apartment.

Emma tried to continue her conversation with Ros, but Logan brought over the vase of flowers and held them up to the screen.

'Pretty, just like Emma,' he said, kissing her cheek. Emma was cross as she didn't want Ros to put two and two together and get the wrong answer.

'I'd better go, Ros. It's great seeing and talking to you. I'll be in touch again soon.'

'Cheerio, Mum. Take care.'

'Nice looking woman,' Logan said. 'Takes after you, I guess.'

Not really wanting to discuss Ros as the conversation might turn to Neil, Emma took the vase of blooms and put it on the windowsill, quickly changing the subject.

'It was sweet of you to bring flowers.'

'I wondered if we could have a special meal this evening. I'm very fond of you, Emma. Please say you will.'

'We often go out for meals. What would make this one so special?' She was puzzled and a little unnerved. Logan seemed different this evening.

He came closer, putting his arms around her.

'I'd like us to be an item, Emma. I

think you're attracted to me and it must be pretty obvious how much I like you.' He bent his face to her and she couldn't avoid his lips meeting hers. She pushed him away and he let her go, looking puzzled. 'I want to have a relationship with you. You're a very attractive woman, good company and intelligent. I thought you liked me.'

She was relieved to have been released from his grasp.

'I do like you, Logan. But what you don't know is that I'm married,' Emma said.

He didn't seem fazed by that.

'But you're here and he's not, right? You've been out with me on several other occasions. We could give it a go, couldn't we?'

'No,' Emma said. 'You see, I'm still in love with my husband.'

He backed off then.

'So I'm just a ship passing in the night for you.'

Emma shook her head.

'I don't see it like that. I think of you as a friend.'

'But that's all?' Logan stared hard at her.

'Yes,' Emma said, 'that's all.'

Emma felt upset when Logan left abruptly. She'd liked being with him when they'd been out and had wanted him as a friend. Thinking about it, she admitted to herself she'd made mistakes, given him the wrong message and she was sorry for that. He was a good man, but not the right man. They'd appreciated each other's company and she'd found him attractive.

If she wasn't still in love with Neil, could she imagine a life with Logan? It would be exciting with lots of travel, she was sure.

And he was fun to be with and had wanted to spend time with her, unlike Neil who'd appeared to want to spend as little time as possible near her.

But she felt Neil was changing and now appeared to understand he'd neglected her and their relationship.

She wondered what Ros had made of Logan and his familiarity with both her and the flat. Would she tell her dad or save him from further heartache by keeping it to herself?

Emma decided she could explain properly next time she was in touch with Ros and she had already said Logan was just one of her friends.

Her falling out with Logan made her feel sad, but thinking of Neil and a possible future with him filled her with hope.

An Explanation

Emma was feeling frustrated. She'd sent Neil numerous texts suggesting times to Skype, but he said he wasn't available as he was doing other things. She found it hard to believe he was leading such a busy life. She was worried.

Once again she wondered what Ros might have said to him about Logan. The only explanation for Neil's reluctance to communicate must be that Ros had read more into Logan's arrival at the apartment. She sent a text to Ros saying she must speak to her urgently.

It wasn't long before Ros responded and they were able to see each other and talk.

'Ros, I'm sorry to bother you, but your dad is never available. I don't understand it. I don't know if you realised he and I have been getting on much better since his accident.'

'Oh, what you mean sort of getting back together?'

'I don't know, really. But we do love each other. It's just a case of working out if we want to live with each other.'

'Oh, I see.' Ros frowned.

'What is it?' Emma asked.

'I don't get it. It looked to me as though you had a new man. I told Dad.'

'Why? I told you Logan is, or rather was, just a friend.' Emma was cross with her daughter.

'Mum! He came in and kissed you and he knew your flat. I mean most people don't keep their vases in the clothes cupboard. He obviously knew his way around the place and was familiar with your things.'

'I keep the vase there because I don't have much storage anywhere else. He'd brought me flowers before and seen me get the vase out.' Emma didn't like justifying herself.

'I'm sorry, Mum. I'll have to put it

right with Dad.'

'Yes, you will. And you can tell him I'm not seeing Logan any more.'

'Are you sad about that?'

'I am. He was a good friend, but he wanted more than friendship. He was looking for a serious relationship and, of course, I wasn't. I'm afraid I didn't behave very well.' Emma sighed.

'What do you mean?' Ros's voice was sharp and she looked surprised.

'I haven't dated a man for many years, in fact I've only ever really been out with your dad, and I think I gave Logan the wrong idea.'

'Never mind, Mum, no harm done. I expect he'll be OK.'

Emma felt sure Logan would be all right.

'How is your dad?' Suddenly she was desperate to know.

Ros fiddled with her hair.

'He seems to have gone downhill a bit again, but he's been told he'll be up and down. I expect once he's physically better and can get back to work and normal things, his mood will improve.' She sighed. 'I don't think I helped by telling him about Logan. Maybe when I put that right he'll brighten up.'

'Maybe. Please do it soon, Ros.'

'I'll speak to him straight away. He's up in the bedroom, probably resting and reading. He seems to do a lot of that lately.'

'By the way, how's your work project going?' Emma asked. 'I don't expect you've the time you would normally devote to it, have you, what with overseeing your dad?'

'No, you're right, but I'm coping and have found a solution to a tricky bit I was puzzling over.' She smiled at her mother. 'Things seem to be coming together on my work front and I really don't mind looking after Dad. I'm quite liking being in the house again and the garden's fantastic — not as neat and tidy as you used to keep it, though.' Ros smiled at her mum. 'By the way, I don't suppose you know we've booked someone to do a twice weekly clean.

Dad couldn't do it and I, well, I didn't want to. Look, I'll get on and tell Dad about Logan. Cheerio, Mum. Love you.'

'Love you, too.'

Emma tried to keep busy while she gave Ros enough time to explain about Logan. She hoped Neil would try to contact her, but in spite of checking e-mails and texts every couple of minutes there was nothing from him. Eventually she decided to stop hesitating and tried to contact him again.

She was disappointed when there was still no response from him. There was no longer a reason for him not to communicate with her unless he didn't believe what she had said to Ros about Logan.

Emma had to put Neil to the back of her mind as she had students to teach. They were getting to know each other's ways and Emma found herself looking forward to their company.

She'd asked Hanami to book her a

class with some of the younger pupils and found them lively and fun. They were also more challenging than the older students and questioned her about the use of language. It was good they were doing so. When Gaku and Aimi asked her if she'd like to join their group for tea one afternoon, Emma found herself refusing in case she bumped into Logan, although she couldn't hide away for ever.

★   ★   ★

Several days later she had given up hope of hearing from Neil. She was desolate. There had been the chance they could make things work and she now longed for that more than anything.

But clearly Neil felt otherwise. It was evening and she decided to concentrate on lesson planning and would try to put thoughts of Neil to one side. But it was impossible.

She closed her laptop and sat remembering their happy times together. There was no denying she missed him. She took their wedding vows from the safe and read them again. A knock on her front door startled her.

Emma wondered if it was Logan at the door and hesitated before answering. However, she still considered him to be a friend, so there was no reason she shouldn't at least speak to him.

On the other hand, it could be a neighbour who needed something. Keeping the safety latch in position, she edged the door ajar.

She took a sharp intake of breath.

'Neil! I can't believe it!' She gasped, in utter confusion. 'What are you doing here? Is everything all right?' Emma's mind went through contortions while she imagined catastrophes large enough to bring Neil from his sick bed halfway across the world.

He stood there smiling at her, a case on the floor at his feet.

'Can I come in, please?'

'Of course,' Emma said, opening the

door wide and stepping back. 'I'll take your case.'

Neil crossed the threshold of the apartment closing the door shut.

'Oh, Emma, it's just so good to be with you. I've missed you.'

Neil wrapped his arms around Emma's waist and she reached up and draped hers around his neck.

They held each other lovingly and Emma inhaled the smell of her husband's cologne, clothes and shampoo.

Neither could let the other go and they remained close for several moments before moving their lips to meet the other's.

It was a replication of their early romantic days of kissing passionately, yet there was a difference now.

Emma knew this was what she'd wanted and missed out on during many years of their lives together. A deep and meaningful love which bound the two of them together for ever.

When they eventually drew apart,

Emma was shocked at her feelings for Neil. To give herself time to recover from their loving caress, she moved the case from the doorway and went further into the apartment.

'Why have you come all this way? Please don't frighten me by holding back bad news. Is everything OK, Neil?'

'Judging by my welcome, I'd say everything is more than OK.' Neil took her hand.

Emma couldn't stop staring at him and was pleased he held on to her hand as she wanted the physical contact with him.

'I've been worried, Neil. How are you feeling?'

'I'm OK, fine. I got here without an escort. I only needed help with my luggage, which I limited to one case. I was helped at the airports, and the taxi driver brought the case to your door.' His thumb stroked her hand. He looked around the apartment and raised his eyebrows. 'You said minute, but it's smaller than that!'

Emma shrugged.

'It's the average apartment for one person here. I've got used to it and there's less housework to do.'

'I've come six thousand miles to discuss your household jobs? I don't think so.'

He moved closer to her and Emma thought he was about to kiss her again. Whilst she had no argument with that, she wanted to know what had been on her mind since she'd lost communication with him.

'Just a minute. Please tell me what you were going to say when we were cut off last time we spoke. All sorts of scenarios have been plaguing me and I've been worried. I couldn't bear the thought of something bad happening to you. Just tell me, whatever it is. When I saw you on the screen, you looked so miserable and I thought something must be wrong. Then you disappeared and wouldn't get in touch again.'

Neil let go of Emma's hand and sat up straight.

'I'm really sorry, Emma, I had no idea I'd given you cause for concern. When I saw you, I was heartbroken that I wasn't with you and yes, you're right, I felt utterly miserable and must have looked it. A sort of envy, jealousy, I'm not sure what you'd call it. I'm sorry to have worried you.'

Emma relaxed.

'So you're sure you're doing OK, you know with the depression and everything?'

'I wasn't going to go into all the details as soon as I saw you, but I will now.' Neil took a breath. 'What I was going to tell you was that I've completely reassessed my life. I have taken time to evaluate working away from home, and work pressure, while I've been recuperating.

'I now understand what's important. It's not about what deals I make or the contracts I get at work, it's about the people I love.'

Emma watched his eyes moisten and grabbed for his hand again.

'Was this helped by the group you said you were going to?'

Neil nodded.

'A lot of the people there had no jobs, no money, no motivation to even get up in the morning and go out. It was an eye-opener for me, and I understood how lucky I am to have what I have. I've got money and a job and a beautiful home, but I've also got a wonderful wife and two adorable children and I love you all very much.'

'I know you tried to show that by earning a lot of money and assuring a secure home and future for the three of us, but all we wanted was you with us.'

'Emma I'll go anywhere in the world to be with you. I don't want to be without you.' He stood and paced the small space they were in.

'Do you remember our marriage vows? I will walk with you . . . '

' . . . hand in hand, wherever our adventures lead us,' Emma joined in.

'I'm glad you remember,' Neil said.

'I brought them with me. The vows. I took them from our house and brought them with me.' She picked up the order of service and showed him. 'It was love which joined us together then and it's love which has joined us together again now.'

They were silent for a while.

'Emma, do you mind if I have a wash and change my clothes?' Neil asked.

'Of course not. I imagine you can wash and dress yourself now, can you?'

'You can help if you like.' He winked at her.

'No, it's OK, I'll make us something to eat, shall I? Or would you like to go out?'

Neil's face was serious.

'I'd like to stay here with you, please.' He reached out for her. 'Emma, I'm touched that you brought our wedding vows with you. It was a very romantic and loving thing to do.'

Second Time Around

They sat eating eggs on toast, talking about the children.

'You said it was love which brought us together again. What made us fall in love in the first place? Can you remember?' Neil asked.

'Your handsome face, of course,' Emma said, smiling. 'Oh, and your infectious laugh won me over completely.'

'What, this one?' Neil gave a pseudo-rumble laugh and Emma giggled. 'I thought you were the most gorgeous woman I'd ever met. I still do, you know. I admired your enthusiasm for everything, and your honesty.'

Emma remembered they'd first encountered each other at a friend's party while she was still at sixth-form college and since then had been inseparable until things had started to go wrong and Neil's work had taken over his life.

'What about the man you've been seeing here?' Neil asked. 'Ros told me all about him.'

'I know and I was very annoyed. She got it all wrong. I saw him as a friend, someone to do things with, but after a bit he told me he wanted a serious relationship.'

'I was right to be jealous?'

'Not as far as my feelings went, no. I feel bad about him. He's a nice man and we did things, like shopping at the supermarket.'

'Really? He saw that as a date?' Neil smiled.

'No, we just liked doing ordinary things together.'

'Is that a dig at me?' Neil asked.

'Not at all, but I would like to spend more time with you, not necessarily doing exciting things, just being together. Logan listened to me when I talked. He treated me better than you've been doing over the past few years, Neil. He wanted me to be happy and made an effort to achieve that.

'He didn't hide his feelings and told me about his two wives and how he didn't want to be alone in America with constant reminders of his beloved second wife. Logan brought me flowers and other little gifts and told me I was beautiful.'

Neil nodded.

'I understand. If you give me a chance, things are going to change from now on. I'm going to make sure you are my priority. When you talk I'll listen, and I'll make you happy, I promise.'

'That's my dream, Neil, just what I've wished for. I'll do the same for you. We'll make the most of your time here. How long are you staying?'

'That depends on you.'

'I'll be happy for you to stay for as long as you have leave.'

'Are you sure?'

'Yes. Why are you grinning?' Emma asked.

'Because I'm taking unpaid leave and can stay as long as you.'

Emma was shocked.

'You're kidding! You never take unpaid leave. You don't even take all your paid leave. It's uncharacteristic. In a good way.'

'I'm a changed man. What do you say? May I share your tiny apartment for a few months?'

'We'll share everything.'

'I told Ros how I planned on staying here for a while. She said she'd be pleased for us, but moaned about us not being home at Christmas so I said she should come, too.'

'It sounds as though you were assuming I'd agree to your plan,' Emma teased. 'Is she going to come?'

'She said she has too little leave, just a few days, and anyway she is busy at work.'

'She's very like you.' Emma directed a playful frown at Neil.

'Mmm, we'll have to tell her the priorities in life. We don't want her to be in her forties by the time she works them out. I had to swear her to secrecy about me coming here as she was dying to tell you.'

'She did well — she gave absolutely no hint that you were coming. What about the house? I suppose Ros has gone back to her place as she is no longer keeping you company.'

'No, it's worked out well. I told her she could stay on in the house as her contract on her flat is up for renewal. She seems to love that house. Living rent free will give her a chance to save towards a deposit for a little house or flat of her own. It's a great opportunity for her.'

'We're all winners. Neil, you can't imagine how happy I am you're here.'

     ★   ★   ★

They quickly settled into a routine which suited them both. When Emma was at work, Neil did any domestic tasks which needed doing. He also learned to cook, finding the local fare fascinating and tasty. But they always enjoyed shopping for the ingredients together.

Because they had decided to stay on in Emma's tiny apartment Neil tried hard to keep it neat and clean. The tiny space wasn't a problem and worked well for them. They grew closer and enjoyed their love for each other.

Neil spent time exploring on his own and often found a place for them to visit or a new experience to try together.

One Saturday evening, they returned from a walk around the local area.

'Are you cooking this evening, or shall I?' Emma asked, hoping Neil would volunteer. She was growing to like not being the only capable person in the kitchen and the whole apartment, come to that.

'We could go out,' Neil said.

Emma smiled.

'We've only just come in. Oh, how I

wish we had a glorious bath like we've got at home.'

'It'll still be there, Emma. Yeah, I think you should have a shower and change. We're going out to eat.' He looked at Emma. 'If that's all right with you.'

★   ★   ★

The last place Emma had thought she'd visit in Japan was somewhere like this.

'I can't believe we're in a karaoke bar. Won't Ros and Sam laugh when we tell them about it? I'll take some photos to send to them. They'll think it's hilarious.'

Emma sipped her lemon sour cocktail and looked around the room.

'How did you get Gaku and the others to let us join them?'

'It was their idea,' Neil said. 'When I came to meet you at the college on Friday, they came over and suggested it. I thought I'd keep it as a surprise. Fun, isn't it?'

'It's a great adventure.'

'And we're on it together.' Neil squeezed her hand. 'Come on, it's our turn to sing.' He pulled her to the microphone and they warbled away as Gaku, Aimi and their friends clapped and laughed.

When they'd finished, there was more applause. All too soon, it was time to go home. The whole group agreed it had been an entertaining evening.

'What a pity you've got to go to work on Monday. I like it when you're around,' Neil said.

Emma linked arms with him as they walked home.

'We don't need to be joined at the hip, darling, we're joined by our souls,' she said.

'What a lovely thing to say. I think you're right, you know. We've always been destined for each other — soulmates. I'm glad we realised before it was too late,' Neil said.

'As I said before, it must have been

love which brought us together again,' Emma said.

They scurried home so they could kiss and cuddle in private.

⋆ ⋆ ⋆

The following day, they had a leisurely morning. Neil brought them breakfast in bed and they discussed what to do that afternoon.

'I think I'd like to try your forest bathing, Emma. I've forgotten the Japanese name for it.'

'*Shinrin-yoku*,' Emma replied.

'Can you remember the garden you told me about?'

Emma nodded.

'I've got it on the laptop. Hang on, I'll show you. It's not too far.' The memory of the calmness reminded her of the time she'd been worried about Neil. 'Can I ask you something, please?'

'Of course, anything you like.'

'How are you feeling? I know you're getting stronger physically, but what about mentally?'

'My depression? Don't be afraid to use the word.' He put his arm around her. 'I'm feeling really well since I came here. Obviously Japan has helped me get over my down moments.'

'Oh, nothing to do with being with me, then?' Emma said, hiding a smile.

'Absolutely not, my darling.' The two held each other and cuddled, their breakfast tea cooling beside them.

* * *

Neil felt he benefited from his time in the gardens and one day Emma came home from the college to find something in the corridor outside their apartment. She frowned at it as she let herself in.

'What's that doing outside? Who does it belong to?'

'The bike?' Neil asked, turning from the stove. 'It's mine. I thought I'd take up cycling again. While you're at work and I'm not slaving away at home. If you want to join me, I could get a tandem.'

'No, you enjoy your cycling. I'm glad you've got the bike.'

Neil came over to her and kissed her.

'I won't neglect you, Emma.' He looked into her eyes and she believed him.

'Shall we go out this evening, after we've eaten? I'm making a delicious stir fry with ramen noodles.'

At the mention of the noodles, Emma thought briefly of Logan.

'Sounds divine,' she said. 'You know, I'm really impressed with the way you've taken on things you couldn't do before, or didn't try to do. I'll have a quick wash, but I'm hungry.'

'You always are.'

★ ★ ★

When they'd finished their meal, Neil patted his stomach.

'I need to walk it off. Shall we leave the washing up until we come back?'

They walked to the edge of town, deciding that they'd stop for tea on the way back.

Sitting in the window seat of a café, Emma looked out and was surprised to see Logan walking past.

He was with a middle-aged woman and they were holding hands and smiling at each other.

Delighted to see him looking happy, Emma waved, wondering if he would see her. He looked up at that moment, grinned broadly at her and waved back.

'Who's that? A student?' Neil asked.

'That's Logan,' Emma said.

'What? But he's an old guy.'

'Yes, he's about your age, darling.'

Neil laughed.

'I suppose you're right.' He put down his cup. 'We've come a long way, Emma.'

'We haven't finished yet. And don't forget,' she paused, took his hand in hers and continued, 'I will walk with you, hand in hand, wherever our adventures lead us.'

We do hope that you have enjoyed reading this large print book.

Did you know that all of our titles are available for purchase?

We publish a wide range of high quality large print books including:
Romances, Mysteries, Classics
General Fiction
Non Fiction and Westerns

Special interest titles available in large print are:
The Little Oxford Dictionary
Music Book, Song Book
Hymn Book, Service Book

Also available from us courtesy of Oxford University Press:
Young Readers' Dictionary
(large print edition)
Young Readers' Thesaurus
(large print edition)

For further information or a free brochure, please contact us at:
Ulverscroft Large Print Books Ltd.,
The Green, Bradgate Road, Anstey,
Leicester, LE7 7FU, England.
Tel: (00 44) **0116 236 4325**
Fax: (00 44) **0116 234 0205**

Other titles in the
Linford Romance Library:

THE LOCKET OF LOGAN HALL

Christina Garbutt

Newly widowed Emily believes she will never love again. Working as an assistant in flirtatious Cameron's antiques shop, she finds a romantic keepsake in an old writing desk. Emily and Cameron set off on a hunt for the original owner, and the discoveries they make on the way change both of them forever. But Emily doesn't realise that Cameron is slowly falling in love with her. Is his love doomed to be unrequited, or will Emily see what's right in front of her — before it's too late?

PARADISE FOUND

Sarah Purdue

Carrie's first visit to Chatterham House, where her grandparents lived and worked, becomes an unexpected turning point in her life when her relationship with her boyfriend ends disastrously there; but she meets Edward, a handsome employee who shares her interest in the estate's history. When she begins volunteering at the house on weekends, she feels drawn to Edward — but the icily beautiful Portia seems to have a claim on him, and his only explanation is that it's 'complicated'. Will Carrie decide he's worth risking her heart for?